LAWN

MAZE

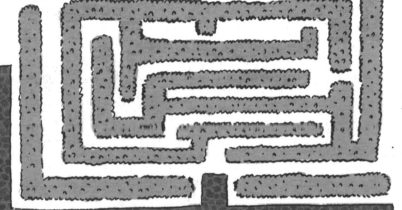

PATH

DRIED-UP
LAKE BED

OLD BOAT
HOUSE

MAP OF
Fallingford

Also by Robin Stevens

Murder Is Bad Manners

A WELLS & WONG MYSTERY

Poison IS NOT Polite

ROBIN STEVENS

Simon & Schuster Books for Young Readers

New York   London   Toronto   Sydney   New Delhi

SIMON & SCHUSTER BOOKS FOR YOUNG READERS
An imprint of Simon & Schuster Children's Publishing Division
1230 Avenue of the Americas, New York, New York 10020

SIMON & SCHUSTER BOOKS FOR YOUNG READERS is a trademark of Simon & Schuster, Inc.
For information about special discounts for bulk purchases, please contact Simon & Schuster Special Sales at 1-866-506-1949 or business@simonandschuster.com.
The Simon & Schuster Speakers Bureau can bring authors to your live event. For more information or to book an event, contact the Simon & Schuster Speakers Bureau at 1-866-248-3049 or visit our website at www.simonspeakers.com.
Book design by Krista Vossen
The text for this book was set in Goudy Oldstyle Std.
Manufactured in the United States of America
0316 FFG
2 4 6 8 10 9 7 5 3 1

Library of Congress Cataloging-in-Publication Data
Stevens, Robin, 1988-
Poison is not polite / Robin Stevens.—First edition.
pages cm.—(A Wells & Wong mystery ; 2)
Summary: In 1930s England, schoolgirl detectives Daisy Wells and Hazel Wong are at Daisy's home for the holidays when someone falls seriously, mysteriously ill at a family party, but no one present is what they seem—and everyone has a secret or two—so the Detective Society must do everything they can to reveal the truth . . . no matter the consequences.
ISBN 978-1-4814-2215-4 (hardback)
ISBN 978-1-4814-2217-8 (eBook)
[1. Mystery and detective stories. 2. Friendship—Fiction. 3. Murder—Fiction. 4. Chinese—England—Fiction. 5. Great Britain—History—George V, 1910–1936—Fiction.]
I. Title.
PZ7.S84555Po 2016
[Fic]—dc23
2015015300

To Boadie

and the M Bs,

with thanks for years of

kindness and friendship—

and for giving Daisy

her house.

FIRST FLOOR

BACK DOOR

MUD ROOM

BATHROOM

LARDER

BILLIARD ROOM

STUDY

SERVANTS' STAIRS TO SECOND FLOOR

KITCHENS

DRAWING ROOM

TO SECOND FLOOR

MAIN STAIRS

PANTRY

CUPBOARD

MUSIC ROOM

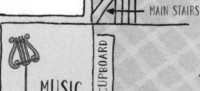

DINING ROOM

LIBRARY

FRONT DOOR

SECOND FLOOR

SERVANTS' STAIRS TO FIRST FLOOR

SPARE ROOM

BATHROOM

LORD HASTINGS'S ROOM

BATHROOM

SPARE ROOM

FROM FIRST FLOOR

TO THIRD FLOOR

SERVANTS' STAIRS TO THIRD FLOOR

AUNI SASKIA'S ROOM

LADY HASTINGS'S ROOM

UNCLE FELIX'S ROOM

MR. CURTIS'S ROOM

THIRD FLOOR

CHAPMAN'S ROOM

BERTIE AND STEPHEN'S ROOM

LAUNDRY ROOM

MRS. DOHERTY AND HETTY'S ROOM

NURSERY

SERVANTS' STAIRS

MISS ALSTON'S ROOM

BATHROOM

The Wells Family Tree

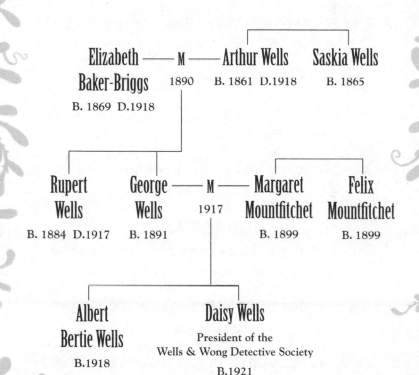

Elizabeth — M — Arthur Wells   Saskia Wells
Baker-Briggs   1890   B. 1861 D.1918   B. 1865
B. 1869 D.1918

Rupert   George — M — Margaret   Felix
Wells   Wells   1917   Mountfitchet   Mountfitchet
B. 1884 D.1917   B. 1891   B. 1899   B. 1899

Albert   Daisy Wells
Bertie Wells   President of the
B.1918   Wells & Wong Detective Society
B.1921

Characters At Fallingford House

THE WELLS FAMILY

Daisy Wells: President of the Detective Society

George Wells, Lord Hastings: Daisy's father

Margaret Wells, Lady Hastings: Daisy's mother

Bertie Wells: Daisy's brother

Felix Mountfitchet: Daisy's uncle, brother to Lady Hastings

Saskia Wells: Daisy's great-aunt, aunt of Lord Hastings

GUESTS

Hazel Wong: Vice president of the Detective Society

Denis Curtis: A friend of Lady Hastings

Miss Alston: Governess to Daisy Wells

Stephen Bampton: A school friend of Bertie Wells

STAFF
Chapman: Butler to the Wells family

Mrs. Doherty: Cook and housekeeper to the Wells family

Hetty Lessing: Maid to the Wells family

DOGS
Toast Dog

Millie

Part One
The Arrival of Mr. Curtis

Something dreadful has happened to Mr. Curtis.

I am quite surprised to realize that I mind. If you had asked me this morning what I thought of him, I should have told you that Mr. Curtis was not a nice man at all. But not even the nastiest person deserves this.

Of course, Daisy doesn't see it like that. To her, crimes are not real things to be upset about. She is only interested in the fact that something has *happened*, and she wants to understand what it means. So do I, of course—I wouldn't be a proper member of the Detective Society if I didn't—but no matter how hard I try, I can't *only* think like a detective.

The fact is, Daisy and I will both need to think like detectives again. You see, just now we overheard something quite awful; something that proves that what happened to Mr. Curtis was not simply an accident, or a sudden illness. Someone did this to him, and that can only mean one thing: the Detective Society has a brand-new case to investigate.

Daisy has ordered me to write what we have found out so far in the Detective Society's casebook. She is always on about the importance of taking notes—and also very sure that *she* should not have to take them. Notes are up to me—I am the Society's secretary, as well as its vice president, and Daisy is its president. Although I am just as good a detective as she is—I proved that last year during our first real case, the Murder of Miss Bell—I am a quite different sort of person from Daisy. I like thinking about things before I act, while Daisy always has to go rushing head over heels into things like a dog after a rabbit, and that doesn't leave much time for note taking. We are entirely different to look at too: I am dark-haired and short and round, and Daisy is whippet-thin and tall, with glorious golden hair. But all the same, we are best friends, and an excellent crime-detecting partnership.

I think I had better hurry up and explain what has happened, and who Mr. Curtis is.

I suppose it all began when I came to Daisy's house, Fallingford, for the three-week Easter holiday and her birthday.

Robin Stevens

Spring term at our school, Deepdean, had been quite safe and ordinary. That was surprising after everything that happened there last year—I mean the murder, and then the awful business with the school nearly closing down. But the spring term was quite peaceful, without any hint of danger or death, and I was very glad. The most exciting case we had investigated recently was the Case of the Frog in Kitty's Bed.

I was expecting Fallingford to be just as calm. Fallingford, for this new casebook, is Daisy's house: a proper English country mansion, with wood-paneled walls and acres of sprawling grounds with a maze and even an enormous monkey-puzzle tree in the middle of the front drive. At first I thought the tree was a fake, but then I investigated and it is quite real.

Honestly, Fallingford is just like a house in a book. It has its own woods and lake, four sets of stairs (Daisy thinks there must be a secret passageway too, only she has never discovered it), and a walled kitchen garden just as hidden as Mary Lennox's in the book. From the outside, Fallingford is a great grand square of warm yellow stone that people have been busily adding to for hundreds of years; the inside is a magic box of rooms and staircases and corridors, all unfolding and leading into each other three ways at once. There are whole flocks of stuffed birds (most especially a stuffed owl on the second-floor landing), a grand piano, several Spanish chests, and even a real suit of armor in the hall. Just like at Deepdean, everything is treated so carelessly, and is so old and battered, that it took me a while to realize how valuable all these things really are. Daisy's mother leaves her jewels about on her dressing table, the dogs are dried off after muddy walks with towels that were a wedding present to Daisy's grandmother from the king, and Daisy dog-ears the first-edition books in the library. Nothing is younger than Daisy's father, and it makes my family's glossy white wedding-cake compound in Hong Kong look as if it is only pretending to be real.

We arrived in the family car, driven by the chauffeur, O'Brian (who is also the gardener; unlike our family, the Wellses don't seem to have quite enough servants, and I wonder whether this also has something to do with the fading state of the house), on a sunny Saturday morning, the sixth of April. We came out of the light into the big dark

Robin Stevens

hallway (stone-floored, with the suit of armor looming out at you alarmingly from the dimness), and Chapman, the Wellses' old butler, was there to greet us. He is white-haired and stooping, and he has been in the family so long that he is beginning to run down, just like the grandfather clock. The two dogs were there too—the little spaniel, Millie, bouncing around Daisy's knees and the fat old yellow Labrador, Toast Dog, rocking back and forth on his stiff legs and making groaning noises as though he were ill. Chapman bent down to pick up Daisy's small trunk with a groan just like Toast Dog's (he really is very old—I kept worrying that he would seize up in the middle of something like a rusty toy) and said, "Miss Daisy, it's good to have you home."

Then Daisy's father came bounding out of the library. *Lord Hastings* is what Daisy's father is called, although his last name is Wells, like Daisy—apparently, when you are made a lord, and sit in the House of Lords in London making laws, you are given an extra name to show how important you are. He has fat pink cheeks, a fat white mustache, and a stomach that strains against his tweed jackets, but when he smiles, he looks just like Daisy.

"Daughter!" he shouted, holding out his arms. "Daughter's friend! Do I know you?"

Daisy's father is very forgetful.

"Of course you know Hazel, Daddy," said Daisy, sighing. "She came for Christmas."

"Hazel! Welcome, welcome. How are you? *Who* are you? You don't look like Daisy's friends usually do. Are you English?"

"She's from Hong Kong, Daddy," said Daisy. "She can't help it."

I squeezed my fingers tight around the handles of my traveling case and tried to keep smiling. I am so used to being at Deepdean now—and everyone there is so used to me—that I can sometimes forget that I'm different. But as soon as I leave school I remember all over again. The first time people see me they stare at me and sometimes say things under their breath. Usually they say them out loud. I know it is the way things are, but I wish I were not the only one of me—and I wish that the *me* I am did not seem like the wrong sort of *me* to be.

"I am Lord Hastings," said Lord Hastings, obviously trying to be helpful, "but you may call me Daisy's father, because that is who I am."

"She knows, Daddy!" said Daisy. "I told you, she's been here before."

"Well, I'm terribly pleased you're both here now," said her father. "Come through to the library." He was bouncing up and down on his toes, his cheeks all scrunched up above his mustache.

Daisy looked at him suspiciously. "If this is one of your tricks . . . ," she said.

Robin Stevens

"Oh, come along, tiresome child." He put out his arm, and Daisy, grinning, took it like a lady being escorted in to dinner.

Lord Hastings led her out of the hall and into the library. I followed on behind. It's warmer in there, and the shelves are lined with battered and well-read leather books. It is odd to compare it to my father's library, where everything matches and is dusted twice daily by one of the valets. Fallingford really is as untidy as the inside of Daisy's head.

Lord Hastings motioned Daisy into a fat green chair, scattered with cushions. She sat gracefully—and there was a loud and very rude sound.

Lord Hastings roared with laughter. "Isn't it good?" he cried. "I saw it in the *Boy's Own Paper* and sent off for it at once."

Daisy groaned. "Daddy," she said, "you are an awful fool."

"Oh, come now, Daisy dearest. It's an excellent joke. Sometimes I wonder whether you are a child at all."

Daisy drew herself up to her full height. "Really, Daddy," she said, "I shouldn't think there's room for *another* child in this house." But she was grinning again, and Lord Hastings twinkled back.

"Now, come along, Hazel. I think we ought to go up to our room."

And off we went.

Lord Hastings kept on playing humorous jokes all that first week. "Daddy," groaned Daisy as she picked a splash of fake ink off her dinner plate on Tuesday, "you are an embarrassment to me." But I could tell, from the way she looked at him as he giggled into his handkerchief, that she didn't mean it. Although the careful, good-show Daisy was still in place whenever her mother was watching, I noticed that her secret side, clever and fiercely interested in everything, kept popping out around Lord Hastings— and that, I knew, meant something. Daisy only shows her real self to people she truly likes, and there are not many of them at all. At dinner that day, though, Lady Hastings was there—and so Daisy was careful to be absolutely proper.

"*Really*, George," snapped Lady Hastings, glaring at her husband.

We all cringed a bit. There was something very wrong between Lord and Lady Hastings this holiday. At Christmas I had thought Daisy's mother perfectly nice, if slightly vague, but this time she was quite different—all brittle and angry at everything. She was still just as tall and blond and glamorously beautiful as she had been at Christmas, but now her beauty was like a porcelain vase that must not be touched. Everything Lord Hastings did seemed to be wrong. Staying in the house with them was a bit like being stuck in the middle of a war, with troops on either side sending shells over our heads. I know all about parents not speaking—at home there are weeks when my mother and father talk to each other through me, as though I'm a living telephone, but this seemed to be something else entirely. Poor Lord Hastings drooped. Hopeful presents of sagging flowers and squashed chocolates kept appearing outside Lady Hastings's room and then were banished straight down to the kitchens, which began to look very much like the inside of a hothouse. Daisy and I ate most of the chocolates for our bunbreaks (Daisy insisted on having bunbreaks during the holiday, "in honor of Deepdean," and I saw no reason to argue with her).

"He loves her," said Daisy, munching an orange cream, "and she loves him too, really, only she sometimes doesn't show it. She'll come round in the end."

I wasn't so sure. Lady Hastings seemed to spend all her time either locked away in her bedroom or on the telephone in the hall, whispering away into it and falling silent when we came too close.

POISON IS NOT POLITE

It was not just Daisy and me who had been turned into hostages of the row between her parents. Daisy's brother, Bertie, who was in his final year of boarding school at Eton, was home for the holidays too.

Bertie looked unnervingly like Daisy—a Daisy stretched out like india rubber and shorn of her hair—but if Daisy fizzed like a rocket, Bertie hummed with rage. He was cross all the time, and as soon as he arrived he began to crash about the house. He had a pair of bright green trousers, an out-of-tune ukulele which he insisted on playing at odd hours of the day and night (according to Daisy he could only play three songs, and they were all rude), and a friend whose name was Stephen Bampton.

I felt very grateful that Stephen was *not* a cross person. He was short and stocky, with smooth reddish hair, and he seemed gentle and slightly sad. He looked at me as though I were a *person* rather than the Orient, and I liked him at once.

I was glad he was there, because this holiday, Fallingford felt foreign—or perhaps it reminded me how foreign *I* was. Bertie jangled away on his ukulele, musically angry, and Lord and Lady Hastings argued, and Daisy went bouncing around the house, showing me secret hiding places and house-martin nests and a sword that had belonged to her great-grandfather, and I began to be hungry for my own Hong Kong house's gluey heat and fake flower arrangements.

Robin Stevens

The last person in the house—apart from the cook and housekeeper, Mrs. Doherty, and Hetty the maid—was Miss Alston, Daisy's new governess. Daisy always had a governess in the holidays when she was back from Deepdean, to help her with all the prep she was given by school and keep her out of trouble—and to help Lord Hastings write letters. "He gets muddled when he tries to do it himself, poor dear," Daisy told me, by way of explanation.

This holiday, though, dull, droning Miss Rose, who we'd had to suffer at Christmas, had quite inexplicably gone away. "With only the briefest telephone call!" said Lady Hastings, as cross as ever. "Really!" Instead, we had Miss Alston.

Miss Alston was, as our Deepdean dorm mate Kitty would have said, a frump. She was the very image of a spinster bluestocking: she wore ugly square clothes without a waist, her hair stood out from her forehead in a bushy, unkempt clump, and she always carried an enormous handbag in ugly brown pigskin. On first acquaintance, she seemed very safe and very dull, but that was misleading. The more lessons we had with her, the more we realized that Miss Alston was not dull at all. She was interesting.

Miss Rose had simply marched us through our Deepdean prep like an army general with no time to waste, but Miss Alston was not like that at all. She had opinions, and ideas.

If we were working on a Latin translation about Hannibal, she would stop to talk about his elephants. If we were learning about water, she took us outside to look at the clouds. If we were reading a Shakespeare play, she asked us whether we felt sorry for the Macbeths. I said yes (though they shouldn't have done it), and Daisy said absolutely not, of course. "Explain," said Miss Alston, and for almost half an hour we both quite forgot that we were doing prep, in the holidays, with a governess.

The oddest thing was that, around the grown-ups, Miss Alston was very different. She was perfectly ordinary. When she wasn't busy with us, she sat with Lord Hastings, drafting his letters and making lists and ordering him yo-yos and fake mustaches from his *Boy's Own* catalogs. He thought Miss Alston deadly dull, just as Daisy and I had before she began teaching us. "She doesn't even laugh at my jokes!" he complained.

"I shouldn't think *that* was a surprise," said Daisy, patting him on the head as if she were stroking Toast Dog. "Mummy, where did you find Miss Alston?"

"Goodness, how should I remember?" asked Lady Hastings, who was busy trying to brush dog hair off her cape. "The agency, I suppose. There was a letter . . . Heavens, Daisy, why must you complain about your governesses? You know perfectly well that I can't look after you."

"Quite obviously," said Daisy icily. I knew what lay

behind Daisy's question. She wanted to understand Miss Alston, and what made her so different—but there was no easy answer to that. Miss Alston kept on being privately interesting and publicly dull, and Daisy and I became more and more curious about her.

L ady Hastings, when she was not mysteriously on the telephone, spent all her time organizing Daisy's birthday party—although it was quite obvious that the party was really going to be Lady Hastings's, not Daisy's.

"A children's tea!" said Daisy scornfully. "How old does she think I am?"

At least Daisy had been allowed to invite guests. Kitty and Beanie, from our dorm at Deepdean, were coming for the weekend, which made me glad. Being at Fallingford was making me think almost longingly of Deepdean's scratchy blankets and smell of washed clothes and boiled food.

On Friday morning, the day before Daisy's birthday, we were in the dining room, and I was halfway through a piece of toast (plum jam from Fallingford's walled garden, butter from its herd of cows) when we heard the growl and crunch of a car on the drive outside.

Daisy sat up, leaving her kipper half eaten. "Kitty!" she

said. "Beanie!" She shoved back her chair and went rocketing out into the hall. I followed her, still chewing and licking jam off my sticky fingers, turned left through the dining room doorway—and went thumping straight into her back.

I yelped and grabbed at her cardigan to stop myself falling over. "Daisy!" I said. "Whatever—"

Daisy had frozen, just like Millie with a rabbit in her sights. "Hullo," she said. "Who are you?"

I craned round her to see who she was speaking to. There, standing in the arch of the stone doorway, was a man. He was quite young for a grown-up, with wide shoulders and a narrow waist, just like a man in an advertisement. He came into the hall, slouching fashionably, and I saw that his face was good-looking, his dark hair very smooth and his smile toothpaste wide. He did not look at all the sort of man who might belong in the front hall of Fallingford House.

The man shone his teeth at Daisy. "You must be Daisy," he said. "The little birthday girl."

"Yes," said Daisy, coming forward to shake his hand with her prettiest smile—though I could tell that she was burning up with fury at being called *little* and burning with curiosity to know who this man was and how he knew her when she had never met him. Daisy, you see, hates to be at a disadvantage with anyone.

Then the dining room door banged open again, and Daisy's mother appeared behind us.

"Mummy," said Daisy lightly, "who is this?"

"Good heavens!" cried Lady Hastings. Her voice had gone very shrill and her cheeks were pink. "How lovely! I wasn't expecting you until later, Denis. Daisy dear, this is my friend Denis Curtis. He's here for your party. Be nice to him."

"I *always* am," said Daisy, beaming up at Mr. Curtis, and I knew that inside she was absolutely seething.

"Your mummy and I are *very* good friends," said Mr. Curtis, who seemed to be under the impression that we were seven.

"Denis is *tremendously* clever," said Lady Hastings, batting at Mr. Curtis's arm with her fingers. "He's in antiques, you know. He knows all about beautiful things. He's going to look at some of the things at Fallingford this weekend. But . . . Daisy, I want all this to be a lovely surprise for your father. You mustn't tell him."

Despite herself, Daisy's eyes narrowed. "Really?" she asked.

"Yes!" Lady Hastings's voice was shriller than ever. "You know how sentimental he can be. But just think how exciting, if some of those horrid old paintings turn out to be worth something after all! I can get rid of them and buy lovely new ones instead!"

This worried me. But what worried me even more was the way Mr. Curtis was smiling at Daisy's mother, and the way he kept his hand on her arm for far longer than was necessary. It was the sort of nasty grown-up thing that I do not understand . . . or understand, but wish I didn't.

Robin Stevens

T hen the drive crunched again—car tires and feet—
but when the door opened, it was still not Kitty or
Beanie. A very large and broad old lady was standing there, her hair all done up in a puff around her head,
a bedraggled fur and several scarves around her neck and
none of her clothes matching.

"MARGARET! DAISY!" she shrieked, waving her arms
and her scarves in the air. "I'M HERE!"

Lady Hastings turned round and looked at her, lips
pinched together. "Hello, Aunt Saskia," she said. "Oh no,
don't bother to ask to come in. Denis, this is Saskia Wells,
George's aunt."

Aunt Saskia came barreling into the hall, shedding
multicolored gloves and bits of fur, and squashed Daisy
against her bosom. She did not seem to have noticed me.

"DAISY!" she cried again. "Where is your brother?
Where is your dear father? And of course, it is your birthday!

Twelve years old! Such a lovely age. I have a present for you—somewhere . . . unless—oh dear, I believe I have left it at Laura and Tommy Bridesnades's house. It was a scarf—at least, I think it was . . . Oh no, wait—here it is!"

And she dragged her hand out of the pocket of her cardigan. Clutched in it was a very small and crumpled square of fabric.

"Isn't it lovely?" Aunt Saskia cried. "It's silk. At least—I think it is. Unless it isn't."

"Thank you, Aunt Saskia," said Daisy. "My birthday is tomorrow. I'll be fourteen."

"Of course you will!" said Aunt Saskia, blinking. "Of course it is. Didn't I say so? And—goodness, who is this? Daisy—Daisy, dear"—she pulled Daisy toward her again and muttered like a foghorn—"there seems to be *AN ORIENTAL* in your hall."

She said it as though I were a bear, or a snake.

"*I know*, Aunt Saskia," said Daisy. "This is *my friend*, Hazel. I *told* you about her. She's a *guest*."

"Really!" gasped Aunt Saskia. "*Such* goings-on! In my day it would never have been allowed."

"I'm sure it wouldn't," said Daisy politely. Aunt Saskia turned to Lady Hastings, and Daisy put her head close to mine and whispered, "In *her* day they shot servants and ate bread made out of wallpaper paste. The past is awful, only old people never realize it."

I felt a bit comforted—but only a bit.

Then Miss Alston came out of the music room, where she had been preparing our lesson. We were to have a day off from prep on Saturday in honor of Daisy's birthday, but up until then we had to work. One of the few similarities between Fallingford and Deepdean is that the grown-ups are all sure that it is dangerous to give children any free time. I think they worry we might get up to something awful.

Miss Alston saw Mr. Curtis standing in the hallway, his suitcase at his feet. For one blink of an eye she stared at him, absolutely frozen. I was looking at her face, and saw the oddest expression on it—a sort of fierce determination, as though she had found something to do, and could not wait to do it. Then her usual blank expression was back. Her fingers tightened around the straps of her fat brown handbag, and she swung round and marched back into the music room again. The movement must have caught Mr. Curtis's eye, and he looked after her, puzzled.

That was odd, I thought to myself. From Miss Alston's expression, I assumed that she knew Mr. Curtis—but Mr. Curtis did not seem to recognize her at all. Of course, he had only seen the back of her head and the set of her shoulders, but that ought to be enough. And anyway, why would a square, serious woman like Miss Alston know a fashionable, smooth man like Mr. Curtis? This made Miss Alston seem odder and more interesting than ever—and made Mr. Curtis more interesting too. I glanced at Daisy, and saw that she had noticed it as well. She was gazing at Mr. Curtis with her vaguest expression. I could almost feel her thinking, *Suspicious*.

Lord Hastings came in from the garden, brushing leaves and cold air off his Barbour jacket. He stared around in astonishment. "Good grief," he said. "Hullo! Guests! Aunt Saskia, how delightful. And . . . who might you be?" He looked at Mr. Curtis from under his beetling white brows and stuck out a fat pink hand for him to shake.

"Denis Curtis," said Mr. Curtis. "Friend of your wife's. Met at a London party a few months ago. She invited me."

There was a smirk in his voice behind the word *friend*. We all heard it. My heart sank. Lord Hastings cleared his throat and didn't look at Lady Hastings. "Splendid," he said hollowly. "How splendid. I hope you'll enjoy your stay here."

"I'm sure I shall." Mr. Curtis's voice glowed with laughter. "Such a beautiful old house. Unique. I can't wait to take the tour." He flashed his teeth at Lady Hastings as he said this.

"Of course," said Lord Hastings. "Of course. Margaret, do—what I mean to say is—I think I shall go and sit in the library for a while. Saskia, will you join me?"

I could feel the misery coming off Lord Hastings as he

led Aunt Saskia into the library, calling, "Chapman! Ho, Chapman!"

I did not like smug, rude Mr. Curtis at all, I decided, and from the way Daisy was vibrating with anger next to me, I could tell that she felt the same. There was something about the way his voice kept nearly laughing, as though he was telling a private joke, and the way Daisy's mother's cheeks were turning pink . . . Something was Going On.

The front door creaked open again, and everyone in the hall turned.

"Hello?" said Kitty. "We did knock, but no one came. Beanie couldn't lift her case, so it's still outside. I say, are we late?"

For a while I thought that the house party might be complete—but then, just after we had all finished lunch (cold chicken and new potatoes, with a splendidly oozing rhubarb trifle for dessert), the last guest arrived. He flashed up to the front door in a blaze of glory in a silver car with a nose like a space rocket, and leaped out, leaving the engine still running, waving his arms and shouting. It was Lady Hastings's brother, Daisy's uncle Felix, and he was just as young and glamorous as his sister.

There had been so many rumors about him at Deepdean—that he was a secret agent, that he had saved Britain single-handed, twice, and received a letter from the king thanking him—that when I saw him it was as though I was looking at a character from a book. It did not help that he looked alarmingly like one of the better-looking heroes from a spy novel. His blond hair was slicked back, his suit was perfectly pressed, he had a gorgeously bright silk square in his buttonhole and a little glittering monocle screwed into his left eye.

He left the car for O'Brian to take round to the old stables and dashed up the front steps, where the four of us were standing (Kitty goggling the way I wanted to, and Beanie saying, "*Ooh!*" in excitement), bent down and kissed Daisy's hand. "Hello, Daisy," he said, winking at her.

"Hello, Uncle Felix," said Daisy, curtsying and winking back.

Uncle Felix seemed to know the right thing to do at all times. He kissed my hand as well, and Kitty's and Beanie's, and Kitty got quite giddy (I nearly did too). Then he went rushing through Fallingford greeting the others. He thumped Toast Dog's and Millie's behinds, punched Bertie lovingly on the shoulder, shook hands with Stephen, gently kissed Lady Hastings's cheek, clapped Lord Hastings on the back, and bowed to Aunt Saskia. Mr. Curtis, though, only got a very stiff and distant handshake—and a very assessing look. Watching them together made me see again just how wrong Mr. Curtis was. They were both as handsome as each other, but Mr. Curtis was all brash and rude and ugly inside, while Uncle Felix seemed to glow in a way that made you want to stare and stare at him.

Mr. Curtis sauntered away, muttering something about looking at paintings upstairs, and Daisy stood on tiptoe and began to whisper crossly into Uncle Felix's ear. I knew she was telling him the story of Mr. Curtis's arrival. He raised an eyebrow—even his eyebrows were elegant—and said something in a low voice.

"He told me not to worry," Daisy whispered when she came back to stand beside me, the wrinkle that always appears when she is concerned by something showing at the bridge of her nose. "He says it's nothing. Uncle Felix is very rarely wrong, but all the same . . . *you* know."

I nodded. It had not *sounded* like nothing.

"At least he's here now," Daisy went on, gazing after her uncle as he climbed the stairs to his room. "He'll make sure that everything's all right . . . At least— oh, I don't like it! Why didn't he believe me just now? It's not like him at all!" She folded her arms across her chest and scrunched up her nose more than ever. I didn't know what to say.

I was not surprised that Uncle Felix should be distant with Mr. Curtis, however, I found it odd that Uncle Felix's usual good manners deserted him with Miss Alston, as well. They met in the hallway, when Miss Alston came to collect us for afternoon lessons: the moment Miss Alston caught sight of him she went all uncomfortable and stiff. Her awkwardness seemed to infect him, and they shook hands like automatons, Uncle Felix squinting through his monocle and Miss Alston sticking her chin out.

"Daisy's uncle, I presume," said Miss Alston coldly.

Robin Stevens

"Delightful. If you'll excuse me—come along, girls . . ."

She strode away into the music room, and we had to follow. I looked back and saw Uncle Felix with his eyebrow raised, staring at nothing. He seemed quite amused, although I could not see the joke. Was Miss Alston really immune to his charm? It made her seem stranger than ever. I had the feeling that they did not like each other—but why? It was yet another mystery in what was becoming a very mysterious weekend.

That evening, Daisy, Kitty, Beanie, and I dressed for dinner in the nursery on the third floor. This is where Daisy sleeps—and where we were all staying during our visit. It was very odd, putting on our best shiny dresses in such a shabby old room: the patterned wallpaper is peeling off in strips, the rag rugs are frayed, and the bedframes are battered, as though they've been beaten with hammers. Candlelight from candles in holders shone on our faces and arms, and made our dresses look soft and faded. Daisy's was rose shot silk, and I could feel the rest of us coveting it, me especially—even though rose makes me look ill and pale, like a goblin child.

"Your aunt is very odd, but I like your uncle," said Kitty, brushing out her thick brown hair. "He's awfully handsome."

I caught Daisy's eye, and we smiled at each other. Kitty thinks everyone is awfully handsome.

"Is he really a spy?" asked Beanie. "I know everyone says so, but—"

Daisy made her face very mysterious. "I can't tell you that!" she said. "If he were, I'd be revealing state secrets. I could be *shot*."

"Oh!" Beanie covered her mouth with her hands. "Oh, I don't want you to be shot. I'm sorry."

"Don't worry," said Daisy grandly. "I shall pretend it didn't happen."

I saw Kitty roll her eyes. "I don't know who I prefer," she said, "your uncle, or your mother's friend. They're both quite glorious."

"Mr. Curtis is *not* glorious," said Daisy sharply.

"No, he isn't," Beanie agreed, fumbling as she tried to tie the ribbon at her waist. "He's not nice. He makes me feel . . . wriggly, like looking at a nasty spider. And he bumped into me earlier and shouted at me to *look where I was going*."

I was shocked. Beanie is so small and sweet, and her big brown eyes are so worried, that it is quite awful to imagine anyone being cruel to her.

"Oh, come here, Beans, and let me do it." Kitty dragged Beanie closer to the candle and tried to manage the drooping bow Beanie had tied. "I'm sure you misunderstood."

"I'm sure she didn't," Daisy said to me in a low voice as we clattered down the stairs in our good patent-leather shoes. "I came down the servants' staircase earlier and surprised Mr. Curtis when he thought he was alone on the second-floor landing. He had his nose right up against the old blue-and-white pot that sits on the sideboard outside Aunt Saskia's room. I could practically feel him calculating how much it was worth, and then—he didn't see me behind him—he said something to himself. I think it was 'Ming.' Hazel, I don't like it. I've never even heard of him before, and now Mummy's being all chummy with him and letting him poke around without telling Daddy. How do we know he's not up to no good?"

"Can't you talk to Uncle Felix again?" I asked. "If he—er—could he help?"

"Not if he keeps on behaving the way he did earlier!" said Daisy. "I don't know what's got into him. He's usually very good at listening to me—hardly like an ordinary grown-up at all."

I felt more curious than ever about Uncle Felix.

"We shall just have to watch Mr. Curtis this weekend," Daisy went on. "It *may* be nothing, like Uncle Felix said. But if he's wrong—well, I don't want to discover it too late. Mr. Curtis can't do anything if we keep our eyes on him. Yes?"

"Yes," I said. "Do we tell Kitty and Beanie?"

"No!" said Daisy. "They'd only spoil things. Detective Society *only*."

"Detective Society only," I repeated. Inside, I glowed.

Was Mr. Curtis up to something? I wondered as we went into the dining room. I wasn't sure—but Daisy and I were on top-secret Detective Society business again, and we would find out.

VIII

There was candlelight at the dinner table too, shining softly on the men's shirtfronts and all the lovely food heaped up on silver dishes. Chapman served us, his brown-spotted hands trembling slightly, so the potatoes and vegetables on my plate were splashed in sauce, but I didn't mind—although Lady Hastings exclaimed quite crossly when some of it fell on her lovely bright green gown.

Uncle Felix was being very jolly. He sat telling uproarious jokes to Bertie and Stephen—and Stephen, who had been so nervous he could hardly hold his fork, relaxed, straightened his back and even began to laugh. I was watching this approvingly when Uncle Felix suddenly glanced over at *me*, his eyes sharp and blue, just the way Daisy does when she is truly considering someone.

I flushed red and looked down at the napkin on my lap, and when I looked up next he was pulling a face at Daisy, as though he had never been watching me at all. Daisy kept her face very prim and straight until Lady Hastings turned away to Mr. Curtis; then she made the most marvelous monkey face back at Uncle Felix. Uncle Felix and Daisy were two of a kind, I decided. They were each just as hidden as the other.

Aunt Saskia was another matter. She fidgeted in her chair, her scarves billowing about her as she gulped down her wine—and dropped silver teaspoons and salt dishes into her little beaded reticule when she thought no one was looking. I had never seen anyone stealing anything so obviously, and I wondered whether I ought to mention it. Then I saw Lord Hastings looking at Aunt Saskia and sighing, and decided that he knew perfectly well already. I supposed that family was family, no matter what they did.

But of course the person I was really watching was Mr. Curtis. And it was not hard to detect something odd in what he was saying. He went on and on about all the things in Fallingford—but what he said did not seem to match what Daisy had overheard earlier. "That vase on the second floor is a fake," he told Lord Hastings. "Margaret told me that you thought it might be Ming, but I assure you it's nothing of the kind. Quite a cheap replica. And the furniture—in a terrible state of repair! You haven't been caring for it at all. It needs seeing to—though it'll never regain its old value. Terrible, really terrible."

"And I suppose you're volunteering yourself?" asked Lord

Hastings, who seemed to be struggling to be a cheerful host.

"I'm something of an antiques expert," said Mr. Curtis. "If you were interested, then perhaps—"

"I won't hear of it," said Lord Hastings. "They're the family's things, and they'll stay in the family."

He put his hands down on the table, and I could see that as far as he was concerned, that was the end of the matter. But Lady Hastings was looking at Mr. Curtis, and I saw her lips say, *Later*, at him. She still wanted to sell to him, I realized—but what if he was not telling the truth about how much everything was worth? Daisy had heard him say "Ming," and now here he was, saying that the vase was *not* Ming. Was he lying? He must be!

I looked at Daisy, and saw that the nose wrinkle was back again. Had we really stumbled across a plot to con Lord and Lady Hastings?

Someone else was watching Mr. Curtis too. I caught Miss Alston's eyes sliding over to him again and again. Her face remained very calm and proper, as though she didn't much care, but it happened far too often to be a mistake, or idle curiosity. What was she doing?

Mr. Curtis was still talking about all the things he had found at Fallingford, and being extremely rude about their value. Even Lady Hastings's jewels were unfashionably cut, he said, and so worth hardly anything. It made me dreadfully uncomfortable. One of the most important things

Robin Stevens

I have learned is that, in England, the more money you have, the less you mention it—it becomes a funny sort of secret; one that you try to bury under dust and faded clothing. (Even my father, who loves all things English, finds this odd.) But Mr. Curtis did not seem to know this at all. "A new one could be worth fifty guineas at least!" he said triumphantly. "I have one quite similar in my own house. But, sadly, in that state of repair—perhaps only four or five pounds."

Bertie made a face at Daisy, and Stephen looked simply horrified. I quite agreed with him.

"But of course," Mr. Curtis went on, "this is still a fine old house. And it has a delightful hostess. Lord Hastings, your wife is simply a jewel, with a face that could launch a thousand ships." His teeth gleamed in the candlelight as he gave Lady Hastings another nasty, knowing smirk.

"Ah yes," said Uncle Felix as Lord Hastings wriggled uncomfortably in his chair and clutched his knife and fork, "I remember how that story goes. Funny, I don't recall it ending well."

He gave Mr. Curtis a very cold stare through the lens of his monocle, and just for a moment Mr. Curtis wilted slightly. But then he straightened his shoulders, his smug expression returned and he began to speak again. As he did so, I noticed him reaching into his jacket and pulling out a pocket watch. It was a fat gold thing, scrolled round with delicate leaves. Mr. Curtis rolled it carelessly between his fingers while he talked. We all gaped at it, and next to me Stephen muttered something under his breath. When I turned to him, he looked as disgusted as I felt.

"How handsome!" Aunt Saskia was staring at the watch, and her eyes were glinting. She looked as though she wanted to lick her lips.

"Oh—this?" asked Mr. Curtis jauntily. "A memento. I do like having beautiful things around me."

"Do you indeed?" asked Uncle Felix, in his most silky voice.

They stared each other down across the table. Everything had suddenly become very tense.

"Goodness!" cried Lady Hastings. "What *has* got into you all? We ought to be celebrating. Let's have a toast. To the party! May this weekend be absolutely perfect!"

Everyone raised their glasses and drank (the four of us girls had Robinsons squash, and had to pretend it was wine). I looked around as we did so, though, and saw everyone staring not at Lady Hastings but at Mr. Curtis. Lord Hastings was red in the face, Uncle Felix was pale and cold as he gazed through his monocle, Miss Alston was looking without seeming to again, Bertie was huffing with indignation, Stephen was still pale with disgust, and Lady Hastings was misty with a kind of cloying fondness that I hated to see. Only Aunt Saskia was staring at something else: Mr.

Curtis's watch, balanced next to his plate. I looked at them all and thought that this weekend would not be perfect at all. On the contrary, it seemed as though it was going to be quite awful. Or, as I could feel Daisy thinking next to me, very interesting indeed.

IX

After dinner the men stayed in the dining room to smoke, and the women got up and went into the drawing room. Bertie and Stephen sat with the men, but although we four had been allowed to play at being grown-up at dinner, it was very clear that we were no longer wanted with either the men or the women.

"Can't you go and play, Daisy dear?" asked Lady Hastings, waving her hand vaguely. "The grown-ups want to talk. Miss Alston, make them play."

"That's quite all right, Mummy," said Daisy sweetly. "We can look after ourselves. We'll play hide-and-seek."

"Oh, if you're sure?" Lady Hastings was clearly glad to clear us from her mind. "But play *quietly*."

"I shall look in on them from time to time." Miss Alston stared at us sternly, her handbag held against her stomach like a shield. I wriggled a bit under her gaze. I knew that Daisy was Up to Something—and I felt, uncomfortably, as though Miss Alston might know it too. Her oddness came through to me stronger than ever.

"Beanie, you count," said Daisy, once Lady Hastings and Miss Alston had retreated into the drawing room—Miss Alston giving one more searching look back at us as she closed the door. "Now, you heard what Mummy said, we must be quiet—and that means staying upstairs, on the second and third floors. Don't come back down to the first floor, otherwise she'll be fearfully cross. All right?"

I knew at once that Daisy was getting Kitty and Beanie out of the way for whatever she had in mind. Beanie nodded obediently, looking excited, and Kitty, who had opened her mouth to argue, sighed and closed it again. I could tell that Kitty wished she could be sitting with the grown-ups, listening to gossip—but Beanie wanted to play, and so Kitty would not disappoint her. It really was awfully clever of Daisy—as usual.

We all climbed the stairs to the second-floor landing, and then Beanie stood facing the stuffed owl on its pedestal, put her hands over her eyes and began to count in a very carrying whisper. Kitty sighed again, looked at Daisy and scampered off toward Lady Hastings's room and the front of the house. Daisy seized my hand, winked and dragged me very loudly up the main stairs, which creak and echo awfully.

But when we reached the nursery landing, we carried on running, across the hallway and down the servants' stairs again. The back stairs are not exactly a secret passageway, but all the same, no one ever seems to think of using them apart from Daisy. They are not for *us*, they are for Mrs. Doherty and Hetty and Chapman, and they are dark and steep and cold. We crept down very quietly, on our tiptoes, hardly breathing, with our hands over our mouths to stop ourselves giggling. It was lovely to be doing something secret with Daisy again.

We came out next to Lady Hastings's room and tiptoed past Beanie, who was still counting. (Beanie needs all her concentration to count, so while she is doing it she is quite oblivious to the rest of the world. It was sharp of Daisy to have suggested her as the finder: Kitty might have noticed what we were up to, but Beanie, never.) Then we crept down the main stairs into the soft light of the hall, with its ticking grandfather clock and worn old paintings on the faded red walls. We tiptoed over to the closed dining room door and stared breathlessly at each other. I could hear deep men's voices through the wood.

Daisy grinned at me. "Good work, Watson!" she whispered. "The first part of our mission is complete. Now, on to the second. By my calculation we will have at least fifteen minutes before Beanie even begins to suspect that we've broken our word and aren't hiding somewhere on the top two floors—fifteen minutes that I mean to make the best possible use of. It's clear from what he said at dinner that

Mr. Curtis is *highly* suspicious. All that rot about the Ming being a fake . . . Don't you agree?"

Now, it is true that Daisy sometimes hares off after the wrong scent, too fast to be altogether decent—but in this case I found myself agreeing with her. I did notice, though, that she was not mentioning how worryingly interested Mr. Curtis was in Lady Hastings.

"He is being very odd," I said. "Which might not mean anything, but—"

"Exactly," said Daisy, as if I had backed her up entirely. "If even *you* think so, then we must be onto something. I don't like him, and I don't like him being in my house. Mummy is sometimes not very bright about people, and in this case I don't trust her judgment at all. As I said before, he must be watched—and this game gives us the perfect opportunity to do so. If someone finds us, we can just say, perfectly truthfully, that we're hiding. And if we aren't found, we may be able to observe Mr. Curtis doing something compromising. He ought to be coming out of the dining room soon, after all. All right?"

I looked at her. Daisy gets very protective about the things that are hers, and I thought she had hit on it when she had said, *I don't like him, and I don't like him being in my house.* But it was still the most interesting potential case we had come across for weeks—if this wasn't worth investigating, nothing was. And, after all, I told myself, whatever happened, *this* case would be safe. It could not possibly turn into a murder.

"All right," I said cautiously.

"I don't know yet," said Daisy, "but I think he's liable to steal something, don't you, or trick Mummy into giving him something awfully valuable? Snooping around our lovely things and then making out they're worth nothing. Well, Mummy might fall for that, but I won't! Whatever he's planning, we must assume that he's going to do it this weekend, while he's here for the party. All we need is enough evidence to take to Uncle Felix, before he can get away with it. Therefore I need you to get under that cupboard immediately. I'll get under the table here, and we'll watch and listen for all we're worth."

I looked at the cupboard. The space underneath it looked fearfully small. "Daisy—" I began. But of course, Daisy was already hiding, and naturally she had chosen the hiding place with more space. I had no choice but to squeeze under the cupboard.

I found it very dark and furry with dust, and extremely close. I lay there miserably, the smell of the men's cigars drifting out through the closed dining room door, mixing with the dust and tickling its way up my nose.

Every time I even moved, Daisy hissed at me like a goose, and by the time the door opened and ten shiny black shoes came trooping past my face, I was thoroughly cross. Sometimes being part of the Detective Society is not enjoyable at all.

"Billiards?" asked Lord Hastings in his big round voice.

"Not for me," said Mr. Curtis, his mirror-polished shoes pausing just in front of my nose. "I've got things to do."

"Not business?" asked Uncle Felix, in his lightest, coldest tones. "I hope you won't be telephoning at all hours . . . You're at a party, you know. You must remember to enjoy yourself."

"Oh, you mustn't worry about that." Mr. Curtis oozed smugness. "I always remember to enjoy myself. And I promise you, I shall have no use for the telephone. Everything I need is here in Fallingford."

I twitched, and the cupboard creaked around me.

"I don't like your tone—" Bertie began hotly, and then stopped, as though someone had put their hand on his arm.

"Shh!" I heard Stephen say. "Bertie, don't."

"Indeed," said Uncle Felix. "Nothing to get upset about. Well, Curtis, we shall leave you to it. Come on, George, Bertie, Stephen. Billiards."

They walked away, and I heard Lord Hastings say in what was supposed to be a whisper, "That man! If he wasn't a guest in my house . . . How *does* Margaret know him?"

Uncle Felix murmured something, and they were gone.

Mr. Curtis was left alone in the hall. His shoes paced to and fro across the faded hall carpet. I wiggled my head forward a bit so I could see Daisy, crouching under her table. She made a cross face at me that I knew meant *Stay put*, and so I drew my neck back in again, groaning quietly.

Then the drawing room door sighed open, and a pair of thin high heels came tapping across the stone floor and onto the carpet next to Mr. Curtis's shoes.

"Denis," said Daisy's mother quietly, like a breath out.

"Margaret," said Mr. Curtis, just as quietly. "Meet you. Nine fifteen. Library."

"Yes," whispered Daisy's mother, and then the library door itself opened, and out came Miss Alston's blocky brown shoes.

"Oh, what a surprise," she said, stopping. "I was looking for the girls, to make sure they really *are* playing hide-and-seek."

"They quite clearly aren't here," said Lady Hastings in annoyance. "Really, can't you keep them under control? Whatever do I pay you for?"

"You are quite right," said Miss Alston blandly. "I do apologize." But although her mouth was saying the words, I could tell that this was not at all what she meant. She went striding off toward the billiard room—but again, I felt that she was doing quite the opposite to what she wanted to. Under all her properness, Miss Alston was just as curious about seeing Lady Hastings and Mr. Curtis together as we were.

Robin Stevens

But for now the scene seemed to be over. Lady Hastings clicked back to the drawing room, and Mr. Curtis muttered, "Whiskey!" and hurried back into the dining room.

I couldn't bear to stay squashed under that cupboard for another moment. I kicked and heaved my way out, bumping my head in the process, and then flopped forward onto the carpet, panting like a fish. Almost before I had time to blink, Daisy was next to me.

"Did you hear?" she hissed.

"I don't see how I could have missed it," I said, and spat out a ball of dust.

"Exactly! Quick—into the library, before Alston comes back and sends us to bed! We must be ready for the rendezvous."

I paused. There was suddenly a little twinge in my stomach. Yes, I had heard everything that Daisy had—but I wondered if it had meant exactly the same thing to the two of us. Mr. Curtis was up to no good . . . but I also knew that sometimes grown-ups went into quiet rooms together for very different reasons. What if *this* was one of those times? Was this a mystery the Detective Society ought to be investigating?

"Daisy . . . ," I said. "Are you *sure?*"

"Hazel," snapped Daisy. "*Do you want to catch Mr. Curtis being a criminal or not?*"

I couldn't argue with that.

Across the hall we went, and into the library. As I opened the door, the warmth from the fire came up against my face like a blush. It was empty, and Daisy motioned toward the heavy curtain draped across the window alcove at the back. We crept in (hiding *again*, I thought sadly), and Daisy pulled the curtain closed. Then we sat there, with our fronts warm and our backsides very cold, waiting to see what was going to happen. Daisy flicked the curtain back a little way so we could peep through, and bounced a bit with excitement, but I was nervous. I couldn't stop worrying. What if I was right?

We were not waiting long. The door opened and in came Mr. Curtis, his face horribly smug and his hands jammed into his pockets. He looked cheerful, but all the same he started like anything when the door opened behind him.

"See?" Daisy hissed to me. "A guilty conscience!"

It was only Daisy's mother, though. She slipped into the

library, hugging her fur around her as though she were cold.

"Now, *be vigilant!*" Daisy whispered into my ear in the half dark behind the curtain. "We must remember *everything* he says to her so we can tell Uncle Felix afterward."

But there was not much to remember. Lady Hastings and Mr. Curtis merely stared at each other with great big round eyes, without saying anything. If Mr. Curtis meant to trick her into giving him the Ming vase on the landing, this seemed an odd way to go about it.

"My darling," said Mr. Curtis. "My darling . . ." And then he took hold of Lady Hastings and kissed her vigorously.

I nearly laughed. Grown-ups look so odd and ugly when they kiss, and Mr. Curtis and Daisy's mother were being so enthusiastic about it.

But then I looked at Daisy.

Her hands were over her open mouth, and her eyes were open too, as wide as they could go. She was staring and staring at her mother and Mr. Curtis, and tears were trickling down her face and onto her curled-up fingers.

I had never seen Daisy cry before. I didn't think she had tears in her, the way ordinary people do. But as soon as I saw her, I realized that this was extremely serious. This was Daisy's mother, and Daisy's mother was married to Daisy's father. She was not supposed to be kissing other men in libraries. She was not supposed to be kissing other men at all.

The library door banged open again and Bertie burst into the room. Stephen was just behind him, and I had a snapshot of his shocked, freckly face, mouth open almost as wide as Daisy's, before Bertie roared, "MOTHER!" and Lady Hastings and Mr. Curtis leaped apart as though they had been electrocuted.

"Bertie!" gasped Lady Hastings. "Mr. Curtis was just—"

The door banged open again, and Uncle Felix came striding in. "Margaret, are you in here?" he called. "I want—what's this?"

"I was having a quiet word with Denis," said Lady Hastings. "Bertie interrupted us."

"A quiet word, was it?" asked Bertie, face burning. "Don't talk such nonsense, Mother. You've done this too many times. If it were up to me I'd—oh! Come on, Stephen. Let's leave these idiots to it." And he turned and shoved his way out of the room, looking ready to crumple up with rage.

Stephen followed him, darting one last shocked glance back at Mr. Curtis as he did so. *Poor Stephen*, I thought, *caught up in the middle of this! And poor Daisy too.* She was still weeping.

Uncle Felix stared from Lady Hastings to Mr. Curtis, then back again, and I could see him understanding everything.

"So, Margaret," he said. "What were you *really* doing?" He suddenly sounded quite dangerous.

Robin Stevens

"I don't see what it is to you," said Mr. Curtis. "It's a free country."

"For one thing," said Uncle Felix, "I happen to be Margaret's brother. And for another—I'd like to know more about you, Mr. Denis Curtis. Which antiques house do you work for, again—was it Christie's?"

Mr. Curtis froze. "*None* of your business," he snarled, all politeness gone from his voice. "I didn't say. And I'll thank you to move out of my way!"

He barged out of the room—very rudely, I thought, hating him more than ever. Lady Hastings was left standing alone beside the sofa, hugging herself with her arms again and looking forlorn.

"Sometimes you're horrid," she said to Uncle Felix. "Why do you always have to go poking your nose in?"

"Margaret, listen for a moment. That man—he's not the sort of person you ought to be associating with. I strongly suggest you reconsider having him in the house."

"Oh, don't be so tiresome," Lady Hastings snapped. "Just because he's my friend! This is my home, and you can't tell me what to do in it."

"He needs to go, Margaret!" said Uncle Felix—but Lady Hastings had already stormed out. He groaned and ran his fingers through his hair, and then he strode out after her. We were alone.

Daisy was still crouched behind the curtain, gulping, her

face covered in tears. I didn't know what to do. She'd had a shock—I remembered vaguely that people in shock were supposed to have cold water poured over them, but I didn't have any cold water on hand.

"Daisy," I said, trying to be encouraging. I knew I couldn't speak about what we had just seen. "Didn't you hear? It sounds as though Uncle Felix is suspicious of Mr. Curtis after all! We might really be onto something!"

Daisy sniffed. There was a short silence. "Hazel," she said in a very small voice, and she crawled out from behind the curtain, "I think you may have a point."

The library door crashed open again.

"THERE you are!" cried Kitty crossly. "See, Beanie? I told you they'd be hiding down here! You beasts! Come on. Miss Alston says we have to go to bed."

D aisy climbed the stairs to the nursery—but her mouth was pinched and her fists were clenched, and I could tell that she was still going over and over what we had seen in the library.

"Are you all right, Daisy?" asked Beanie, peering at her. "Your face is red."

"I'm quite all right," said Daisy, snapping to attention. "The library was hot, that's all."

"We saw Mr. Curtis just now," said Kitty. "He was looking awfully cross about something. Is *he* all right?"

"Ha!" said Daisy, before she could stop herself. "I mean, I'm sure he is."

"He had that glorious watch of his out again," Kitty went on. "Your Aunt Saskia was there too, and she was simply ogling it. It was quite funny to watch. She was like a cat staring at a bird!"

"But it's Mr. Curtis's!" said Beanie, shocked.

Kitty sighed, and even Daisy grinned briefly. Beanie is so beautifully honest that she thinks the rest of the world must be too.

"Excited about your birthday tomorrow?" asked Kitty. "I simply adore birthdays. So many presents!"

"I suppose so," said Daisy vaguely. "The birthday party, though—ugh! A children's tea! I don't know how old Mummy thinks I am."

Of course, she wasn't really cross with her mother because of the birthday tea. It was the library, I knew—and I felt awful for her. She couldn't even breathe a whisper about it to the others—if Kitty knew, we would be hearing about it all weekend, and the whole school would know as soon as summer term began.

So I was not at all surprised when Daisy made an excuse to leave Kitty and Beanie changing in the nursery while we went to brush our teeth in the third-floor bathroom.

The upstairs bathroom is just as faded as the rest of Fallingford. Its white porcelain is all cracked, and there's a rusty ring around the edge of the clawed bath. The tap drips, and a green stain wriggles all the way down from the top of its chain into the hole where the water runs away, like the ghost of a worm.

"Are you all right?" I asked, as soon as we had bolted the door behind us and turned on the water. It gulped and hissed, and quite drowned out our voices to anyone trying to listen.

Daisy waved her hands and sat down on the edge of the bathtub. "Of course I am," she said. "Don't concern yourself about *that*. I've been considering what we have discovered so far, and it seems to me that since Mr. Curtis is in this house for nefarious purposes, what we saw in the library today is simply more evidence of his wicked plans. He has clearly decided to trick my mother into falling in love with him so she'll believe that all our nice things are worthless—and as I said before, Mummy is often not at all bright about people. We must consider her the victim, and Mr. Curtis the very cunning criminal."

"But, Daisy," I said. "It still *happened*."

"Well, yes, it *happened*, but it doesn't *mean* anything, Hazel. As soon as we unmask Mr. Curtis for the villain he is, Mummy will come to her senses—what she has of them—and go back to Daddy. So, you see, it's more imperative than ever that we uncover enough evidence to show to Uncle Felix, and we do it as quickly as possible."

I looked at Daisy. Her eyes were glittering and her cheeks were pink. This was Daisy with A Plan. But although I agreed with her about Mr. Curtis, I was still terribly worried. I could see that she was up to her old tricks again—trying to make the evidence fit the way she hoped it would. But no matter the reason why Mr. Curtis had kissed Daisy's mother, he had still done it, and Daisy's mother had kissed him back. I remembered all the arguments between Lord and Lady Hastings that week, and knew that, whatever Daisy said, the situation between them was very serious indeed. What if Daisy's mother wanted to run away with Mr. Curtis? What would Daisy do then?

"So, Watson," said Daisy, "we must absolutely watch Mr. Curtis like hawks tomorrow. We can't let him out of our sight!"

"But it's your birthday!" I said.

"Never mind birthdays! Some things are more important. Besides, I've had plenty of birthdays already."

There was a sudden banging on the door.

"Let us in, Squashy, you horror!" shouted Bertie. "Don't be a fool, come out! What are you doing in there?"

"Brushing our teeth, of course!" shouted Daisy. "Oh, all *right*. We're coming out."

She unlocked the door, and we went out onto the landing. Bertie was there, arms crossed, and beside him was Stephen. I blushed to be seen coming out of a bathroom by two boys, but Daisy merely sniffed and looked unconcerned, as though she had just emerged from a ballroom.

"You're a queer fish, Squashy," said Bertie when he saw us. "I heard the two of you talking. What was it about?"

"You, and how vile you are," said Daisy rudely. "Poor old Stephen, forced to spend time in your odious presence. Now clear off and stop sticking your nose in."

Bertie scowled and made a horrible face at her, but

Stephen smiled at me. I still felt rather awkward, but I smiled back.

"Why does he call you Squashy?" I asked curiously when we were back in the nursery. Beanie, who was already in bed, waved at us.

"According to *him*, I was a fat baby," said Daisy. "That isn't true, of course. I was perfect. And anyway, *he* had to wear an eye patch for his squint until he was ten. He thinks it's terribly amusing to call me . . . that name . . . *now*, but if he ever gets engaged I shall call him Squinty in front of his fiancée and we'll see if she still wants to marry him then."

"Come along, Daisy," said Miss Alston. She was in the nursery, waiting for us to get in bed so she could say good night.

"Miss Alston," said Kitty, as Daisy put on her nightie and got into her bed, "what do you think of Mr. Curtis? Don't you think he's dreamy?"

"I'm not paid to think anything of anyone," said Miss Alston, pursing her lips. "He is the friend of my employer, and that is that. Good night, girls."

She put out the lamp and went out of the door, and Daisy blew out the candle on her bedside table—a funny three-legged thing which had once been green but was now not much of anything. Then Daisy rolled over so that her nose was against the peeling yellow wallpaper (a circus scene, with elephants and lions and ringmasters chasing each other in circles), and began to breathe as though she were asleep—but I knew that she was still very much awake. Kitty crept into Beanie's bed to whisper with her, and I wanted to speak to Daisy—but was not quite sure what I should say.

I thought of my bedroom at home, all smooth and white, with the fan going round and round soothingly above my head, and the voices and chiming glasses from my parents' drinks parties drifting up the stairs. Here the blankets itched, and though I had three of them I still shivered. The nursery walls were all crooked, the house creaked and grumbled, and something shrieked outside. I remembered the first night I had spent here, when I thought it was a baby, but Daisy told me it was only a fox. All at once I longed to go home.

It was odd, because I should have been enjoying myself—it was the holiday, and I was with Daisy, after all—but I was feeling more and more homesick. Suddenly I couldn't wait until Daisy's party was over.

Robin Stevens

Part Two
An Investigation and a Birthday Tea

The next morning I was woken by something sitting very heavily on my stomach.

I gasped and opened my eyes.

"Hello, Watson," said Daisy, leaning over so that her hair tickled my face. "It's my birthday. Come on, get up—we've got a villain to unmask. Look, I brought provisions."

She dropped an apple and an English muffin, leaking butter and honey, onto my front. A shining oily patch spread across my nightie before I could snatch it away.

"Daisy!" I said, eating the muffin in large sticky bites to get rid of it. "What's this?"

"Prebreakfast breakfast." Daisy bit into a muffin of her own. "I would have thought you of all people would understand. Detectives need sustenance."

"How *early* is it?" I asked. "Happy birthday, by the way."

"Not very," said Daisy. "Half past seven. Oh, come on, Hazel, I've been up for hours and *hours*, and so have Hetty and Mrs. D. But listen, we must begin *at once*. As I came up the stairs past the second-floor landing I heard movement in Mr. Curtis's room. We can't let him just wander about without being watched!"

This morning Daisy looked *happy*—glowing with it, not at all like the girl I had seen behind the curtain last night. I thought I knew why. She had taken all the real things that had happened yesterday, and in her head she had turned them into the wooden parts of a puzzle. I was still worried for her, but I couldn't say anything. If this was how she had chosen to deal with what we'd seen in the library, I couldn't stop her—it was her birthday, after all.

Our talking had woken Kitty and Beanie.

"Whatever's wrong?" grumbled Kitty, raising herself up on her elbows and peering about the nursery. "Why are you awake?"

"Happy birthday!" cried Beanie, leaping out of bed and standing up on her tiptoes like a small ballerina. "I didn't forget!"

Daisy suddenly sat up, digging her knees into my stomach and scrambling over me to get to the window above the head of my bed. She wriggled her fingers through the bars and squashed her face out as far as it would go. "Look!" she cried.

We clambered up next to her, Beanie wriggling curiously and Kitty still grumbling at how early it was, and through the black crosshatch of the bars we saw Mr. Curtis, in tennis shorts and an Aertex shirt, jogging easily across the gold-shining morning lawn. He looped round the maze, which cast a long dark shadow over the paler grass, and leaped over the gravel pathway, with its clipped box hedges and little stone urns. At the woods by the lake he turned and began to jog back toward the big oak and the walled garden. We all watched him go.

"Why are we looking at Mr. Curtis?" asked Beanie.

"Ooh, *Daisy*, do you have a pash?" said Kitty, giggling.

"*Hardly,*" said Daisy. "I only mean—whatever is he doing up so early? It isn't normal." She elbowed me in the ribs as she said this, and I winced.

But just then someone else appeared on the lawn, coming around the back of the house from the stables where the cars are kept.

It was Lord Hastings. He had his Barbour jacket on, a snapped-open rifle hanging over one arm, and Millie leaping along at his heels. Toast Dog was panting and struggling behind them. As he stumped through the grass he looked absolutely *right*, in a way that Mr. Curtis didn't. He raised his hands to his mouth and gave a "*Halloa,*" and Mr. Curtis reined himself in. They approached each other—and suddenly I couldn't help feeling nervous.

Mr. Curtis had the swagger back in his step. He said something that we couldn't hear (Daisy scrabbled for the catch and pushed the window open a little—we were still too high up and far away to make out any words), but it looked like what he said was swaggering as well. Lord Hastings's round face turned beet red. He jerked his chin up, just like Daisy does when she is truly furious, and bellowed, so loud that we could hear almost all of it, "ENOUGH, SIR! I have been trying to . . . but now I . . . leave this house IMMEDIATELY! . . . staying another night under . . . who you are!"

I could hardly believe it. Lord Hastings was making Mr. Curtis leave Fallingford!

I expected Mr. Curtis to be angry, or upset, at what Lord Hastings had said—but on the contrary, he threw back his head and laughed. Then he said one more thing, turned on his heel and jogged away. Lord Hastings was left standing alone, clenching his fists and panting like Toast Dog.

"Lord!" said Kitty. "What was that about? Will Mr. Curtis really have to leave? Poor man!"

"*Poor*—!" Daisy started. Then she remembered herself, and made her face go very innocent. "I can't think what it could be. I'm sure it's just a boring grown-up thing. Let's go down to breakfast."

I was halfway through my third piece of toast and marmalade—and trying to keep my nose away from the foul, fishy-smelling kipper Daisy was dissecting behind the pile of presents arranged for her by Miss Alston—when Lord Hastings came bustling into the dining room. He was still slightly red-faced and grass-stained, but he seemed determined to be cheerful. "Daughter!" he cried when he saw Daisy. "Happiest of birthdays! Aren't you going to open your presents?"

"Thinking about it," said Daisy. "Perhaps at tea. Mummy hasn't given me anything, I see."

"I'm sure it'll come later," said Lord Hastings, head turned away as he piled his plate with bacon and eggs.

As he was speaking the door swept open again, and Aunt Saskia wafted in. She lost a scarf on the door handle and an earring under the sideboard (Chapman had to bend down with an arthritic crunching of knees, and fish it out), and her nasty furry wrap came undone and almost slipped off her shoulders. I saw with disgust that it had a face like a squashed cat's. I thought I must be imagining things, but it really did have little shining eyes and a flat nose, and whiskers. I shall never understand the English even if I live to be a thousand.

"Good morning, Aunt Saskia," said Lord Hastings. "Bertie, do pass the salt."

Bertie passed it, making a face at Daisy from behind his hand. Just then there was a shriek from the kitchens. We all jumped and stared nervously at each other, and I wondered what other awful thing could have happened. Mrs. Doherty stuck her head through the door, looking flustered.

"Apologies," she said. "Hetty found another rat in among the flour. It's the third this week!"

"I wasn't frightened!" called Hetty from beyond her.

Chapman frowned crossly, and I could tell that he did not approve. *Fetch the poison*, he mouthed at Mrs. Doherty.

"Yes—the arsenic in the hall cupboard," said Lord Hastings, busily salting his eggs. "A big tub of it. Bring it out, Mrs. D., and dispatch the rodents immediately."

"Very good, Lord Hastings," said Mrs. Doherty, and she backed out of the room.

At that moment Mr. Curtis came in, his hair gleaming wet from his after-run bath. "Happy birthday, Daisy," he said.

"Thank you," said Daisy graciously, but the bridge of

her nose wrinkled up as she said it, and I could tell that she was surprised. So was I. What was Mr. Curtis doing, coming down to breakfast so casually after what we had seen? Should he not be packing his bags? Lord Hastings was clenching his hands around his cutlery, and his teeth around the mouthful of egg he had just taken, but he didn't say anything. I wondered if he was as surprised as we were.

Miss Alston murmured something about getting things ready for our lessons and slipped out of the dining room, but I scarcely noticed her go. I was too fascinated by Mr. Curtis.

He seemed determined to brazen it out. He took a plate of food and sat down at the table, setting his lovely gold watch down next to his right hand. Aunt Saskia gazed at it as though she wanted to eat it—I quite saw what Kitty had meant yesterday.

"Further to our discussion," he said to Lord Hastings, "I don't find it convenient to leave before this evening. If you could ask your man to take me to the station for the nine oh six train I should appreciate it."

I thought Lord Hastings might snap his knife, he was gripping it so hard.

Bertie looked at him, and then back at Mr. Curtis, and scowled. "I do think," he said loudly, "that there isn't enough arsenic used in this house. The rats seem to get *everywhere*."

"It must be a terrible problem," said Mr. Curtis, and he took a defiant bite of his bacon. I swear I saw him smirk at Bertie.

Bertie puffed up with rage, and Stephen had to put a hand on his arm to calm him. Chapman nearly dropped the coffeepot.

"Have a care, Chapman," said Lord Hastings, jumping. "Curtis, O'Brian will have the car ready by eight this evening. Please be prompt."

"I shall," said Mr. Curtis, still with that smirk on his face. I could tell that he thought he had won. He stood up, stretched, and sauntered out of the dining room.

By my wristwatch, Daisy left a careful minute before she put down her knife and fork and said, "Lovely breakfast, Chapman. Do thank Mrs. D. Kitty, Beanie, you finish up. Hazel and I will be waiting for you outside." She kicked me under the table, and I gulped down my last marmalady mouthful and said, "Yes, I'm finished."

"Good work, Hazel," said Daisy, and we ducked out of the dining room before Kitty could protest.

Mr. Curtis was still in the hallway. He was peering at one of the paintings, an old one in a dark frame. It was of a lady, very fat and nude, holding up her arms and beaming, and Mr. Curtis was staring at it in the same way as Aunt Saskia had stared at his watch. Once again, he didn't look like a person who thought that the things in Fallingford

Robin Stevens

were worthless. He didn't even notice us come out of the room—he was studying the painting closely, scribbling something down in a little notebook. Daisy nudged me. Was that notebook *evidence?* Could we work out a way to read it?

But then I noticed something else. We were not the only people in the hall. The door to the music room was cracked open, and Miss Alston was peeping out. She was staring at Mr. Curtis with an odd expression on her face—very still and thoughtful, as though she were taking in everything about him. What was she doing?

Daisy had seen her too. She frowned, and looked from Mr. Curtis to Miss Alston, and back again. Then the dining room door slammed behind us in a sudden breeze, and Mr. Curtis jumped back from the painting. The scene, whatever it had been, was over.

Now all Daisy and I had to do was work out what it meant.

When we went into the music room, Miss Alston startled slightly, and tucked something into her big brown handbag. It looked like a bit of paper. "Girls!" she said. "You oughtn't to be in here. You'll spoil the surprise of the games later."

"Yes, but we know there are going to be games anyway," said Daisy, "so it's hardly surprising."

"Manners, Daisy," said Miss Alston, looking severely at her. "That isn't a very nice thing for a young lady to say."

"Nice!" said Daisy. "Who wants to be nice?"

"You do," said Miss Alston. "Or at least, you ought to seem as though you do."

It was such a very true thing to say about Daisy that I gaped. And I wondered what that bit of paper had been. It was not just Mr. Curtis who we needed to watch, I thought. It was Miss Alston as well.

A ll morning we followed Mr. Curtis as best we could. We had to carry on doing birthday things with Kitty and Beanie, and playing the games that had been set up by Miss Alston. Although they were not a surprise, they were quite good, especially as most of them were memory games that Daisy was sure to win. During bunbreak, though (buttery shortbread, baked by Mrs. Doherty), we came upon Mr. Curtis on the second floor, peering at something on a table. It was one of Lady Hastings's heavy old jeweled brooches. I saw his face, and there was greed all over it.

"Oh, goodness, I forgot I left that there. Is it worth anything?" Lady Hastings asked behind him.

"Well . . . ," said Mr. Curtis. "Such an unfashionable cut, in such a setting . . . You might be able to get a pound or two for it, perhaps. There isn't the demand for such things these days!"

Again, what he was saying and how he was looking did

not match up at all. It was highly suspicious.

Just before lunch we saw him go past the door of the music room, out into the garden, and although the sun had gone in and the sky was fat and gray with cloud, Daisy suddenly decided that the one thing in the world she wanted to do was go and play in the maze. Kitty, who hates getting her hair wet, predictably said no (I wished I was allowed to agree with her), and Beanie loyally said she would stay with Kitty, so it was only Daisy and I who rushed out of the front door a few moments later. We turned left onto the front lawn, and saw that we were in luck. Mr. Curtis was actually disappearing into the maze.

"After him!" hissed Daisy—and down the lawn we dashed, into the close, green-spiked tunnels. I could hear Mr. Curtis up ahead, stamping along, but every path looked just the same, and just as wrong, and I wasn't sure which way to go. Daisy, though, seized hold of my hand and dragged me forward, privet pulling at our skirts and socks, until I was sure that Mr. Curtis would hear us or—worse—run into us.

But Daisy, of course, knew exactly what she was about. She came to a sudden stop, inches from a flat green wall—and there, on the other side, I heard voices.

"What are you doing here?" Mr. Curtis sounded furious. All the oil had gone out of his voice. "I was going to meet—"

"Margaret?" Uncle Felix sounded perfectly silky. "I don't think that's a terribly good idea under the circumstances, do you?"

My heart began to thump, and I tried not to look at Daisy. I had been hoping to avoid any more mention of Mr. Curtis and Lady Hastings.

"Are you *warning* me?" asked Mr. Curtis.

"Nothing so gauche. However, if you choose to take it as that, I won't contradict you. I think it would be best for all concerned if you left this house as soon as possible. If you stay—well, you might not like what happens."

Mr. Curtis snorted. "You can't touch me," he said.

"Can't I? I think I can. You see, I know what you're really here for."

There was a very cold silence on the other side of the hedge.

My heart leaped into my mouth. What did Uncle Felix mean? Was he simply telling Mr. Curtis that he knew about him and Lady Hastings? He could be, but to me it sounded like something more.

"And what's that?" asked Mr. Curtis, all bluster. I could almost see him throwing back his shoulders and jutting out his well-defined chin.

"You know," said Uncle Felix. His voice made me shiver. "You know very well."

Daisy was elbowing me frantically, mouth wide open.

Mr. Curtis cursed filthily, and I felt the privet wall in front of us shiver. Then off he went like a shambling bear, growling away to himself and making the maze around him shake.

He was very easy to follow—though as we ran after him, everything seemed doubled and confused. I heard our footsteps, and his—and what I thought must be Uncle Felix's, just to the left of us, or just behind. But then I heard Uncle Felix to our right, muttering to himself. It gave me a horrid jump. Who had we heard before?

At last we burst out of the maze—and there, coming down from the house toward it, was Lady Hastings. So it had not been *her* in the maze! She was peering up at the sky and teetering along in her high heels.

"Where's Mr. Curtis?" I gasped. We heard a noise, and turned—but it was not Mr. Curtis we saw coming out of the maze. It was Miss Alston again. Her face looked flushed and her handbag was dangling from her arm. The mystery was solved.

"Daisy!" she said. "Hazel! There you are. Where did you get to?"

Then Mr. Curtis burst out of the maze, panting and red-faced. He saw Miss Alston and started. I am quite sure (although she covered it very well) that she started too, as if guilty. What had she been doing?

Mr. Curtis was looking very angry indeed. He glared at

Robin Stevens

Miss Alston and then pointed a furious finger into her face, so that she had to step back.

"I know what you are," he growled. "I know what you're here for. Well, you'll have to do better than that if you want to catch me out. Hah!"

Then he saw Lady Hastings, and stared from her to Miss Alston, as though he wasn't sure how much she had heard—and what she would make of it.

"I don't know what you are talking about," said Miss Alston steadily. "Girls, do come inside. I believe it is beginning to rain."

Of course, we had to be good and follow her, dodging raindrops as we went, but my heart was jumping about with excitement. What had Mr. Curtis meant about Miss Alston? We had seen her watching him suspiciously earlier, after all. Was this something to do with that bit of paper she had been hiding? Daisy poked me, and I could tell that she was having exactly the same thoughts.

The stone walls of the house closed in around us with a chill I could feel through my dress. Kitty and Beanie were hovering about in the hall, Beanie looking shy and out of place, and Kitty very cross. "You've been ages!" she said to us accusingly. "We're bored. I say—"

But just then the dining room door swung open, and Mr. Curtis and Lady Hastings came out. They must have got in from the garden through the French windows. It was odd seeing them again so soon—I stiffened, and Daisy clenched her fists tight against her skirt.

"Give me a week's warning, at least—I can't simply go—" Lady Hastings was saying heatedly. Then she saw us, and stopped with a jerk. "Girls," she said. "Daisy. Miss Alston, didn't I just now tell you to keep them amused?"

"My apologies, Lady Hastings," said Miss Alston colorlessly. "Girls, time for another round of birthday games, I think."

"Oh goody," said Daisy, not taking her eyes off her mother.

Lady Hastings blushed. Then she cleared her throat and said, "Marvelous. Lunch is at one. Oh, and, Daisy—happy birthday."

"Thank you, Mummy. Are you going somewhere?"

"No," said Lady Hastings, who had suddenly seen something very interesting on the ceiling. "Poor Mr. Curtis has been called away on business, and I was persuading him to stay. You must have misunderstood."

"Oh dear, I must have," said Daisy. "How silly of me."

We followed Miss Alston into the music room for our games, Daisy craning round behind her as subtly as she could to look at her mother and Mr. Curtis. "Hazel!" she hissed in my ear. "Mr. Curtis is becoming more and more bold. We have to keep a watch on him—there's no telling what he might do next!"

Robin Stevens

I thought I could guess. Mr. Curtis was leaving that night, and he wanted Lady Hastings to go with him. If Daisy used even half of her detective skills on the problem, she would know that. But it was her birthday, and you are allowed to pretend certain things on your birthday.

"We will," I said, and I reached out and gave her fingers a squeeze.

Daisy squeezed back. "Good old Hazel!" she said. "I knew I could count on you."

After lunch (only a few cold cuts of meat and salad, as the tea was planned for later) we had yet more birthday games. This time it was Sardines, and even Bertie and Stephen were persuaded to join in. We went in and out and up and down the wriggling many-cornered corridors of Fallingford, losing each other and finding each other again, and bumping into Chapman and Hetty as they tidied rooms and prepared Daisy's birthday tea. In one round I was squashed behind a fat leather sofa that was shedding horsehair through splits in its lining, when Stephen crawled in behind me. He looked miserable and pinched.

"Hello, Hazel," he whispered. "What's up?"

"Nothing," I said. Then, "This is a funny sort of birthday for Daisy, isn't it?"

Stephen made a face, and all the freckles on his nose wriggled. "*Awful!*" he said. "That man, Mr. Curtis—I don't like him. He's the reason Bertie and Daisy's parents have been arguing."

"I know," I said, my stomach lurching.

"I hate it when parents argue. It seems like such a waste. You see, my father—my father's gone. So when I see mothers and fathers rowing—I wish they wouldn't, that's all. They don't know what might happen."

I wanted to hug him, but I was not sure whether Stephen was a hugging sort of person, or whether I was the sort of person who hugged boys behind sofas in empty rooms, so I said, "Oh dear!" and gingerly patted him on the arm.

"It's quite all right," said Stephen thickly. "It was years ago. Though I don't feel much like playing Sardines anymore, somehow. What say we stop for a bit?"

I stood up with great relief, because the back of the sofa had smelled like pressing my face against a very wet and dirty horse (Daisy tried to take me riding once, for five minutes, so I know what I'm talking about), and took a big gulp of fresh air. Stephen went over to the window, hands in pockets, sauntering like a cat. Then his back stiffened.

I ran over and peered out too. We were in the little box room on the second floor, filled with old, broken furniture. It looks down onto a patch of front lawn and the gravel walkway with its stone urns and little ornamental bushes. Mr. Curtis and Lady Hastings were standing there. Lady Hastings was wrapped in her fur, and Mr. Curtis was holding his gold watch. The clouds had gathered up even more, angry and dark, and it was raining hard. I wondered what on earth they were doing outside, instead of coming into the dry—I knew that Lady Hastings absolutely hated getting wet. But then I saw why they weren't thinking about being rained on. They were arguing again. Snatches of their conversation floated up to us.

". . . rather sudden, Denis," said Lady Hastings.

"I don't see that it is," said Mr. Curtis. "Your husband . . . and we wouldn't want . . . bring your jewels and the painting I told you about."

"But, Denis, dear . . . can't—" began Lady Hastings.

"If you don't," said Mr. Curtis, in quite a different, hard voice, "I shall tell your husband . . . up to. We'll see . . . thinks. How do you like that?"

Lady Hastings gasped and clutched her fur tightly around her shoulders. "Denis!" she cried.

"You have until after tea to make a decision," snapped Mr. Curtis. "And if not—well!"

He stormed back toward the front door and, with a gasp, Lady Hastings chased after him.

Around them, the rain had become a downpour, and I could hear grumbles of thunder far away in the hills. I turned and looked at Stephen. He was rubbing his cheek, as shocked as I was. "What did he mean?" he asked. "Do you think . . . ?"

Robin Stevens

"I don't know," I said. I felt very frightened. "Don't tell Daisy or Bertie."

Stephen nodded. "Mum's the word," he said. "But what if—"

"He won't," I said. "He can't. He'll be gone after the tea party. He said so."

I wished I really felt so confident. What if Mr. Curtis did do something awful? I had a horrible feeling that things were about to go very wrong. "Can't we go down and find the others?" I asked.

At the point where the main stairs turned, we paused. Below us the hall was empty, but we could see the wet tracks where Mr. Curtis and Lady Hastings had rushed through. The game had come through here too, and the hall was looking very disheveled. All the cupboard doors were hanging open, the carpets were scuffed up, and some-one had brought the stuffed owl down and put it in the umbrella stand.

"Hurry!" I hissed. Mr. Curtis must be nearby, and I didn't want to meet him at all. We scampered down the stairs, and I dived for the safety of the library. The door closed behind me, and a moment later Stephen came running in after me.

"Sorry," he panted, wiping his forehead. "I panicked. Froze up—nearly caught!"

Beanie popped her head out from behind a chair. "Hello!"

she said cheerfully. "What are you doing out of hiding?"

"*Beanie!*" groaned Kitty, crawling out from under an occasional table. "You aren't supposed to give us away!"

"Have we won? Oh, have we?" asked Beanie.

Then Daisy emerged from an impossibly small nook in the corner of the room—Beanie jumped and squeaked, and said, "How did you get there?" and the game seemed to be over.

Robin Stevens

At ten to three by my wristwatch the dinner gong rang; it sounded wobbly because Chapman was the one striking it.

"Ooh," said Beanie. "Tea!"

Daisy didn't say anything—just smoothed down her skirt and patted her hair. I could see that she was dreading it. "Tea!" I said to her encouragingly.

"Yes," she said. "Tea. Spiffing."

Beanie and Kitty took her at her word—but as we went out into the hall I caught hold of her hand and squeezed it again, and Daisy squeezed fiercely back.

As we went into the dining room, I felt a sort of sadness come over me. I couldn't explain it, because all the electric lights in the room were blazing and there was the most gorgeous spread on the table—an enormous teapot, surrounded by lovely pillowy cream cakes, and jellies in four different colors, and jam tarts, and ham, and boiled eggs, and muffins, and a fat chocolate cake with *Happy Birthday Daisy* piped in white icing with presents all round it. But the rain was slicing down outside the windows, harder and harder, and although Chapman had tried to tidy up and draw himself up tall, his hair was not quite combed and he had a speck of something pale on his lapel. His hands, as always, were shaking. I knew that really, although things looked so bright, they were all wrong underneath. I didn't know how to behave among all these strange English people—more than ever, I wished I could go home to Hong Kong, where everything was safe and understandable, and even the rain was warm. Jellies were all very well, but they weren't half as good as moon cakes.

"Girls!" cried Lady Hastings, spreading her arms dramatically. In her bright green dress she looked like a fashion plate come to life. "Welcome to our little gathering in honor of dear Daisy's birthday. Thirteen years old today!"

"I'm fourteen," said Daisy.

"Oh, are you?" asked her mother vaguely. "Really? Well, I suppose it does happen."

"It tends to," said Lord Hastings. "Especially when you aren't looking."

Lady Hastings shot him a glare. "As I was saying," she went on, "I thought it would be the most lovely fun to have a *proper* children's tea—for us to serve ourselves, just the way we used to when *we* were young."

"I don't suppose you remember being young, Daisy," said Uncle Felix, winking at her, "at your great age. What a long time ago your youth was!"

"Oh, good heavens, do be *quiet*, Felix!" complained Lady Hastings. "I'm *trying to explain*. We're all serving ourselves, and it will be such fun, and I want you all to absolutely stuff yourselves silly. This is a *proper children's tea!*"

I was not sure what a *proper children's tea* was, or how it was different from tea in our house dining room after school. Huddled in the doorway, Daisy, Kitty, Beanie and I all looked at each other, mystified, and Daisy rolled her eyes. Her cheeks were very pink again, and her eyes were shining—but I didn't think it was with excitement.

However, the grown-ups and Bertie and Stephen seemed far more pleased. As the rain outside worsened, they all crowded round the long table, jostling for space next to the teapot. Aunt Saskia, who was draped in even more silky scarves than usual, pounced on a plate of cream cakes as though she hadn't eaten for at least a decade, while Lord Hastings (in a rather nicer tweed jacket that didn't go with his mud-stained trousers) snatched up an enormous slice of ham. In fact, the only grown-up who held back was Mr. Curtis. He slouched fashionably, hands in his well-cut suit pockets, as though he had not a care in the world—but I got the distinct feeling that he didn't want to go anywhere near Uncle Felix or Miss Alston. Something, I sensed, was *happening*, something to do with what we had overheard in the maze. Would Mr. Curtis leave before we had the chance to find out what it was?

I suddenly remembered the scene between Mr. Curtis and Lady Hastings that Stephen and I had witnessed. I shifted uncomfortably. What if Mr. Curtis didn't leave on his own— or what if he did, and told Lord Hastings all about him and Lady Hastings, just as he'd threatened? What would Daisy do then? I hadn't told her about it yet—I couldn't bear to.

"Let me know when the chaos has died down a bit," Mr. Curtis drawled, and threw himself into one of the squashy chairs that Lady Hastings had made Chapman drag in from the library and set out in a semicircle near the door. Then he pulled the gold watch out of his pocket and rolled it around in his hands absentmindedly. For a moment Aunt Saskia paused with a jam tart halfway to her mouth. As she gazed at the watch, her eyes were round with desire; then she turned back to the tea table.

There was still an absolute scrum at the tea table; I was aching to join in—it seemed a long time ago that we had been given those cold cuts of meat—but I knew I could not until Daisy gave the word. Good china clattered and clinked (I saw Chapman wince), and everyone seemed to be talking and snatching cups up at once.

"Stand back! *I* shall be Mother and pour the tea!" cried Lady Hastings gaily. "Let *me*!"

But everyone seemed to be ignoring her and fetching their own tea—apart from Chapman, who moved as far away from the tea table as possible.

"Oh, at least fetch a cup of tea for Mr. Curtis!" she said to no one in particular. "Here—oh—"

"I have one!" Lord Hastings turned to Mr. Curtis with a cup in his hand. It was full to the brim and wobbling—little drips of tea went snaking down its white and gold side—and he thrust it at Mr. Curtis so quickly I thought it really would spill.

Mr. Curtis snatched it rudely, without looking up or thanking Lord Hastings, and swallowed it down in one enormous gulp. Then his face twisted. "This tea is disgusting," he snapped. "Ugh! Foul!"

"What a pity," said Lord Hastings. His lips were pursed, like Daisy's when she is trying not to laugh, and he quickly turned away from Mr. Curtis and went back to the tea table.

By this point, although I knew I ought to show support for Daisy, I was almost overpowered by the desire for a jam tart. I could see Aunt Saskia bearing down on the plate again, her eyes glinting and her hands outstretched eagerly.

"Oh, all right," said Daisy, although I had not said anything. "Teatime. Come on, everyone, dig in!"

I heaved the most enormous sigh of relief. All three of us had been waiting for her. Daisy grinned at me, and then she darted forward, swiped my beautiful tart from under Aunt Saskia's nose and presented it to me.

"I saw you eyeing it," she said. "Oh, look at this cake! Chapman, you are a brick." Daisy was making the best of it, I thought, and I was proud of her.

"We know that chocolate's your favorite," said Chapman, patting her on the shoulder with his wrinkly old hand. "Mrs. D. made it specially for you. Happy birthday, Miss Daisy."

We ate and ate and ate, and I got crumbs all down my good dress (so did everyone, even Lady Hastings, but nobody seemed to mind), and I was just thinking that it might be quite an enjoyable party, after all, when the chatter was abruptly stopped.

Robin Stevens

M<sup>r. Curtis coughed. He looked surprised at himself. Then he coughed again, sharply, as though
he were trying to clear something stuck in his
throat. That was what we all thought had happened.

"Shall Chapman—I mean, shall I get you a glass of water,
Denis?" asked Lady Hastings, putting down her cup of tea,
but Mr. Curtis shook his head and put his hand up to his
still-open mouth.

"My tongue," he said thickly. "I feel—" And he actually
stuck his finger between his lips and prodded it.

I was shocked. You simply do not behave like that at a
tea party unless you are a baby, which Mr. Curtis was quite
obviously not.

"Augh," said Mr. Curtis. "*Augh!*" And all of a sudden he
doubled up in his chair, folding himself over like a paper
doll. Then he began coughing again, louder now, until
the coughs became retching noises. It was horrid to listen

to—it made my own throat tickle. Nasty as Mr. Curtis was, it was awful hearing him choking away like that. Kitty had her hands over her mouth; Beanie had hers over her eyes.

When Mr. Curtis sat up again for a moment, his face had gone white and waxy, and he was making the most dreadful groaning noise, mixed in with the retches.

"What is it?" asked Beanie. "What? What's wrong?"

With a cry Lady Hastings rushed toward Mr. Curtis and put her arm around him. He put his hand over his mouth and heaved.

"Quick!" Lady Hastings cried to Chapman. "Fetch Mrs. Doherty and Hetty! Tell them that Denis has been taken ill and is up in his room." Then she pulled Mr. Curtis, still retching, to his feet and guided him out through the door. Chapman, looking almost as waxy-white as Mr. Curtis, tottered after her.

The rain pelted down outside as I stared around at everyone else. Aunt Saskia had her mouth open, and her hands clutched the sides of her face, which looked like a horrid mask. Uncle Felix was standing with his arms folded, his expression very stern. Miss Alston's face was quite blank, but she was clinging to her handbag as tightly as anything. Bertie looked as though he did not know who to be angry at, and Stephen looked as if he might be sick. And then I glanced at Lord Hastings. He was trying to look concerned, just as the host of a guest who has just been taken ill ought to, but underneath I could see a nasty sort of pleased expression that did not suit him at all.

"What's wrong with Mr. Curtis?" Beanie kept whispering fearfully. "Oh, what's *wrong* with him?"

"Shut it, Beans!" hissed Kitty rudely.

What *was* wrong with Mr. Curtis? I wondered. Was he ill? If he was, it was very sudden. We had seen him out jogging that morning, after all. Had he eaten something bad? All I had seen him take was that cup of tea.

I felt a pinch on my hip, and turned to see Daisy widening her eyes at me. It was as though she had held up a sign. *This may be important!* said Daisy's eyes. She was right. Strange things kept happening around Mr. Curtis, as though he were a magnet for them.

"Come on," said Uncle Felix to everyone, as we heard voices and feet on the stairs. "Out, all of you." He flapped his hands at us, shooing us out of the dining room ("I don't see *why!*" complained Aunt Saskia) and then stood in the doorway, looking forbidding. The birthday tea was clearly over. I peeped round his arm and saw the tea things all strewn about and Mr. Curtis's watch and cup still balanced on the arm of the chair he had been sitting in—and then my view was cut off. Toast Dog tried to wriggle his way in to the dining room between Uncle Felix's legs, and Uncle Felix said, "Oh no you don't," and shut the door on Toast Dog's nose. "Mrs. D!" he called. "I need the key to the dining room!"

Mrs. Doherty came flustering out of the kitchens, carrying a bowl of water. "Of course," she gasped. "It's hanging up in the kitchens. But I must just take this upstairs to Mr. Curtis first."

"Daisy, we can't wait. Go and get the key," said Uncle Felix, not moving. "Don't argue with me."

Daisy went, looking bored and don't-care—though I could tell she was fizzing with excitement underneath. When she came back, Uncle Felix locked the dining room door, put the key in his pocket and went bounding up the stairs to Mr. Curtis's room, his long legs taking three treads at a time. I was worried: Uncle Felix was behaving as though something was seriously amiss.

"What is wrong with Mr. Curtis?" repeated Beanie. "Did he eat something bad?"

"My aunt mistook bath salts for sugar once," said Kitty. "She was ill everywhere. The house smelled horrible for days."

"Mr. Curtis hasn't swallowed *bath salts*," said Daisy scornfully. "Don't be silly. I expect he ate something that disagreed with him at lunch—some of that meat was rather old."

Did she believe that? I wondered. One look at her told me that she didn't.

"Oh no!" wailed Beanie. "Will we all be ill?"

"Most likely," said Daisy, who was clearly in a ghoulish mood. "In fact, I think I feel—"

Beanie shrieked, and clutched her stomach. "Help!" she cried, and made a dash for the bathroom. Kitty,

Robin Stevens

rolling her eyes at Daisy, went chasing after her.

"Daisy!" I said. "You know that isn't true. *I* don't feel ill—at least, I don't think I do."

"Of course," said Daisy. "You're right, I may not have been entirely truthful with Kitty and Beanie."

When are you ever? I wanted to say—but I didn't. "So?" I asked.

"So? Hazel, haven't we been saying all day that something odd is going on? Mr. Curtis is obviously here for nefarious purposes, we have established that—this could just be a trick to stop Daddy forcing him out of the house this evening. If he's ill, he can stay on at Fallingford."

"But I don't think he was pretending!" I objected.

"Neither do I, really. But if he isn't pretending—well, that is even *more* interesting. There are all sorts of possibilities, and it is up to us as members of the Detective Society to investigate them further, before we draw any conclusions. What do we know so far? Quick, while we're alone."

"Mr. Curtis has been behaving oddly," I said. "And now he's taken ill—it looked like he was going to throw up."

"But none of the rest of us are showing symptoms of sickness, although we all ate the same things at lunch," Daisy pointed out. "And we all ate the same food at tea just now."

"But Mr. Curtis didn't eat anything!" I said. "He only drank that cup of tea."

"Excellent observation, Watson!" said Daisy. "Good.

Now, that tea came from the same pot that we all had our tea from, and the milk from the same jug. So why is Mr. Curtis ill, when none of the rest of us are?"

Just then Uncle Felix rushed past, pulling on his raincoat and galoshes.

"Are you going out?" asked Daisy.

"Going to find O'Brian and fetch the doctor," said Uncle Felix briefly. "Things look bad upstairs, and the storm's playing havoc with the phone lines. Best not to go alone."

I did not envy him or O'Brian at all. Things sounded awful outside. I could hear thunder kettledrumming away, and the rain hammering against the windowpanes—and every so often the outside of the rattling windows was lit up fiercely white by lightning.

"If we're not back in half an hour, send out a boat—there's a good niece."

Daisy grinned and waved him out, but as soon as the door slammed behind him her face grew serious. Everything had changed—Daisy's birthday celebrations were over as though they had never been. We stared at each other, listening to the pounding rain and the horrid retching noises filtering down from upstairs. It was pitch-black outside now and wild; it felt as though the house was a little wooden box that we were all stuck in together, alone on a deep dark sea.

"What we must do now," said Daisy, above the roaring of the storm, "is get closer, and see what we can discover."

Robin Stevens

VII

Up the twisting stairs we went, and along the second-floor landing, to lurk outside Mr. Curtis's door. We could hear Lady Hastings and Mrs. Doherty fussing about inside. I knew we shouldn't be there—and I knew I didn't want to be. Mr. Curtis kept making those horrid wails and groans—they nearly drowned out the storm outside. Flashes of lightning kept on striking the hallway full of shadows—they made me jump every time.

"Honestly, Hazel," Daisy said, but she did not say it with feeling. I think she was beginning to feel as nervous as I was.

Then Uncle Felix came back with the doctor from Fallingford Village. Unlike Felix, who looked smooth even with rain dripping from his hair and his trousers soaked and muddy, the doctor was fat and bald and flustered, and very out of breath. He rushed past us, saying, "Out of my way, young ladies, out of my way!"

Uncle Felix paused beside us; we both tensed, but he only frowned and wiped his wet monocle on his wet pocket square.

"We left O'Brian in the village," he told us. "Awful weather—he's better off at home. But at least Dr. Cooper's here now."

"What's wrong with Mr. Curtis, Uncle Felix?" asked Daisy, seeing an opportunity. "Will he be all right?"

"Stop angling, Daisy," said Uncle Felix. "I'm not going to tell you anything."

Daisy looked shocked. "But—Uncle Felix!"

"Daisy, this isn't a game. This is serious. Now I want you both to go up to the nursery and stay there until you're told otherwise. All right?" He glared at us through his monocle, now back in his eye, and then jerked open Mr. Curtis's door and strode in.

Daisy was left gasping. "I . . . ," she said. "I don't know what's got into him this weekend! He *never* tells me to go away!"

I thought back to those strange, worrying things that Uncle Felix had said to Mr. Curtis in the maze. *Was* he behaving like a grown-up? Or . . . like a suspect?

"What do we do now?" I asked Daisy. "Go upstairs, like he told us to?"

"Obviously not," she said. "That big Spanish chest over there opens, and there are some lattice bits that make

Robin Stevens

perfectly good air holes. If we hide in there we can stay and listen."

I didn't want to stay at all—but I *did* want to listen. "All right," I said.

We climbed in. Our elbows and knees bumped in the dark, and I felt very hot and claustrophobic. But Daisy was right—there were small holes in the side of the chest that we could breathe through, and almost see out of (if we squinted). Thunder rumbled and boomed, the rain lashed down against the windows, and Mr. Curtis groaned and groaned.

And then his bedroom door opened and someone came bursting out. It was Lady Hastings, and she was simply howling. She held a handkerchief to her face, which had tear tracks all down it, and ran into her room, sobbing. And a few minutes later, just as I was beginning to wonder if I should ever move about freely again, two more people came out after her.

It was the doctor and Uncle Felix, and they weren't running or crying, but they did look very solemn. Uncle Felix pulled the door of the room shut behind them, and they stood close together, facing each other. Daisy elbowed me in the ribs, and I held my breath.

"It is serious, Mr. Mountfitchet," said the doctor. "Very serious indeed. I wish I didn't have to be the bearer of bad news, but I would say that now is the time to . . . to begin preparing for the worst. I have seen several of these cases before: as soon as this stage is reached—the purgings, the convulsions—there is very little hope left."

"*Several* of these cases?" Uncle Felix repeated. "You have a diagnosis, then, Dr. Cooper?"

"Dysentery, I should say," Dr. Cooper replied. "A fairly clear-cut case. The loss of fluids, the stomach pains. As I say, I have seen—"

"Dysentery? You're sure?" asked Uncle Felix, his voice sharp.

"As sure as I can be without a closer examination of the matter—er—evacuated. Anything else would be pure speculation. After all, this is a reputable household."

Uncle Felix's shoulders tensed—and next to me, Daisy suddenly went stiff, as though they had both heard the same invisible sound.

"*What?*" I whispered, as quietly as I could.

"Shh! Wait!" hissed Daisy.

"Humor me," said Uncle Felix. "Take some samples. I can take them up to the laboratory in London tomorrow."

"Tomorrow?" said Dr. Cooper. "I doubt that very much. Fallingford and the surrounding countryside is going to be flooded—and you know that this sort of flood isn't liable to die down for days. And anyway—forgive me for being blunt, but I doubt whether this man has even a few hours left. I simply can't get fluids into him as quickly as he loses them. Any tests will be quite irrelevant."

"Nevertheless, I want you to take them, and give them to me. Is that clear?"

"Yes indeed," said Dr. Cooper. "I only meant . . . Forgive me—I must get back to the patient."

"All right," said Uncle Felix. "Thank you."

He strode off toward his bedroom, and Dr. Cooper ducked back into Mr. Curtis's. As soon as the doors had closed behind them, Daisy burst up out of the chest like a jack-in-the-box. The air opened up above me and I took a grateful gasp. But I couldn't think what Daisy was doing. What if someone came out and caught us?

"Daisy!" I said, crouching half out of the chest.

"Oh, there's no time, Hazel! Quick! We have just been given the most important clue. We must get to the library immediately!"

I decided that this was one of those times where it was important to let Daisy have her way, so I crawled out of the chest and chased after her. She barreled down the main stairs, her feet drumming like the rain, and across the hall into the library. Thank goodness, there was no one there.

When she was inside, Daisy leaped across the room and clawed at the leather-bound books like a tiger. She ripped one off a shelf, threw it to the floor (Daisy adores books, but she does ill-treat them in a most upsetting way) and began to rifle through it. "Here!" she cried. "Look at this!"

I squinted at the open page. It seemed to be from the A section of some sort of medical textbook. *Arsenic Poisoning*, I read.

Symptoms: numbness, nausea, vomiting, and diarrhea (often bloody), convulsions (often violent), severe dehydration, severe thirst, abdominal pain.

Symptoms first present fifteen to thirty minutes after ingestion, beginning with warmth and tightness of the mouth and throat. Nausea and stomach pains follow, after which violent purging begins.

Robin Stevens

Vomiting should be encouraged at the earliest possible opportunity, but cases where the patient has ingested more than four grains are generally fatal. A mere two grains have been known to kill. Death may occur anytime between two and forty-eight hours after ingestion, and is caused by circulatory collapse.

Note: can often be mistaken for the symptoms of DYSENTERY.

I went cold all over. It couldn't be . . . Daisy was imagining things again. Except . . .

Except that none of the rest of us were ill. Except that all the symptoms I had seen—and Dr. Cooper had mentioned—matched those we had just read about. Except that there was a tub of arsenic rat poison in the hall cupboard, and after the discussion at breakfast, everyone knew about it.

Except that it all *made sense*.

I gasped at Daisy, and she looked up at me, her mouth a round O of shocked excitement.

"I'm right!" she cried. "I knew it, the moment Dr. Cooper said dysentery. I've read about this in a book. Hazel, this is *serious*. Mr. Curtis isn't just ill. He's been poisoned!"

I gulped. There was a thick feeling at the back of my throat. The drumming of the rain was so loud that I could hardly hear the inside of my head. It sounded as though it was trying to batter its way into the house. What if we were stuck here? I thought all of a sudden. What if we were flooded, and what if Daisy really *was* right?

"Hazel, this case has just taken a fascinating turn. A real poisoning! And here we are, on the spot, ready to detect it! We must unlock the dining room door now and—"

"There you are!" said a voice behind us.

We both jumped, and Daisy slammed the book shut. Miss Alston was standing in the doorway, her hair bushier and more unkempt than ever. She looked pale and tired.

My heart began to pound. I glanced sideways at Daisy, but her face was giving nothing away. Sometimes I feel as if I'll never be able to appear as cool and collected as Daisy.

"Sorry, Miss Alston," she said, as though she were apologizing for a torn skirt.

"Come on upstairs," Miss Alston said. "Your friends are wondering where you've got to.'

"Oh, all *right*, Miss Alston. We're coming."

We were taken up to the nursery, and there was nothing we could do about it. Investigating the dining room would have to wait.

The rain was beating on the roof above our heads, sounding as though it was about to burst through and drown us all, and Beanie was huddled on her bed, shaking, while Kitty comforted her. "Honestly, Beans," she was saying as we came in. "He'll get better!"

Daisy and I simply looked at each other.

Robin Stevens

Hetty, looking just as tired as Miss Alston, her red hair escaping from her cap in a frizz, brought supper up to us on a tray. It was boiled eggs and toast. "Oh, really," said Daisy in disgust. "We aren't ill. Why are we being sent an invalid's supper?"

"*Daisy!*" said Miss Alston warningly, and Daisy was quiet—but privately I agreed with her. Even though people in stories always lose their appetite when something dreadful happens, in real life it is not like that at all. The worse things get, the hungrier I am. I can't help it. By that time—it was nearly eight at night—my stomach was rumbling dreadfully. I could have eaten another enormous tea.

"But he *will* get better," Beanie kept saying, like one of those dolls with a voice inside. We all pretended we hadn't heard.

Daisy was itching to talk about what we had discovered, but there never was a chance. Miss Alston was always hovering around—just as though she knew, and wanted to keep us here! I thought. It was infuriating.

Then there was a tap on the door, and Miss Alston was called outside. She closed the door behind her, but I heard her speaking to someone—Hetty—in the hallway. Once again, we couldn't go anywhere or do anything without her knowing about it. I stared at the bars on the nursery windows and tried very hard to be sensible and calm. This was not last year again. Mr. Curtis was not dead. We would wake up next morning and look out of the window and he would be jogging round the grounds again. Then he would leave Fallingford as planned, and we would be glad, and everything would be ordinary again.

The door opened again and Miss Alston came in. Her expression was very odd. We all stopped what we were doing and looked at her.

"Girls," she said, "I'm afraid I have some bad news. Mr. Curtis has died."

Robin Stevens

Part Three
Really Truly Arsenic

I wrote up all my case notes so far last night. I knew that we were really and truly on a case—and compared to that, bedtime did not matter at all. After Miss Alston had gone away again, Beanie had proper hysterics, and we all had to crowd round and comfort her and tell her that it was all right; *she* would be all right.

"But what if we die too?" she sobbed. "Kitty, I don't want you to die!"

"Honestly, Beans, it isn't catching," said Kitty.

"But how do you KNOW?" wailed Beanie, and that was another twenty minutes gone.

I crouched on my bed and wrote furiously, because I knew that I had to get it down quickly, before any of it went out of my head. I felt dreadful. If Daisy and I had told someone what we suspected, might we have been able to help Mr. Curtis? After all, he may have been awful, but he had still been a person. And now, *if* we were right about what had happened to him, then someone was responsible for the fact that he was not a person anymore, and that was terrible. I decided that we had to solve the crime, to make up for not speaking out earlier that evening. All the things Daisy and I had seen over the last few days had suddenly become extremely important. Any one of them might mean something, and any one of them might help reveal the murderer.

You see, I had realized something. It was no good hoping that a mystery murderer had crept in from outside, poisoned Mr. Curtis's tea and vanished into the night. I had seen for myself the wet tracks made by Mr. Curtis and Lady Hastings when they came in from the rain on Saturday afternoon— and also noticed that there had been no other such tracks anywhere in the house. No one had come in after them, and no one but the weekend guests and Chapman had been in the dining room when Mr. Curtis had been taken ill. The rain absolutely ruled out anyone but the people inside Fallingford House, I thought, and I felt a bit sick.

There was a murderer on the loose again; and they were very close to us. If we went hunting them, would we be safe?

It was still raining, too. As I wrote I heard the water bucketing down, hammering against the roof above me like fists. Water leaked through into buckets on the nursery landing, *drip-drip-drip* like soft footsteps. What if we *were* trapped

Robin Stevens

here? Fallingford House was on a hill, and Dr. Cooper had said that the countryside around it was flooding. What if the police couldn't get to us? I wrote and wrote, but all I wanted to do was talk to Daisy. If only Kitty and Beanie would go to sleep!

At last Beanie and Kitty were quiet. They were huddled together in Beanie's bed, and Beanie was making little snuffling noises as she slept. Daisy had been pretending to sleep too, but as soon as we heard Beanie's snores she sat up in bed, eyes wide.

Watson! she mouthed. *Detective Society meeting. Outside. Now!* It is a very good thing I have been practicing my lipreading.

I crept out of bed (the old broken floorboard halfway across the nursery groaned, and I made an apologetic face at Daisy), and together we slipped out. We heard snoring from Miss Alston's little room, and a creak as she rolled over in bed.

It was a very cold, early hour of the morning, and the house was a little circle of calm within the howling storm outside. Daisy motioned toward the servants' stairs. In the darkness they looked almost like a secret passage. I imagined us vanishing down them and never coming out—but that was silly, shrimplike behavior, of course. I took a deep breath and followed Daisy carefully down twenty steps. On the twenty-first (I counted) she stopped, and I bumped into her in the darkness.

"Halfway down," she breathed, clicking on her flashlight so that it lit her face eerily. I jumped. "Perfect. Mrs. D., Hetty, and Chapman are asleep. No one else even remembers these stairs are here—Mummy doesn't like thinking about them: she says they're too dirty to bear. So we won't be disturbed. Sit down, Hazel. It's time to go over the facts of the case."

"All right," I said, sitting down on a very hard and uncomfortable stair.

"We know that Mr. Curtis is dead," said Daisy, ticking things off on the fingers of her free hand. "That's quite unarguable. And what we *think* is that he has been murdered. What Dr. Cooper said suggests that he was poisoned. We know there's arsenic in the hall cupboard, and we know that arsenic poisoning fits with his symptoms. That must be the most likely cause. But how do we *prove* it? And if he was poisoned, who did it?"

"If Mr. Curtis was poisoned, I think it must have been someone in the house," I said. "It's awful, but nothing else fits. If he had been poisoned at breakfast or lunch, he would have begun to feel ill hours before he did—so he must have been poisoned at tea. It was raining by then, and we didn't see any wet tracks, did we, the way we would if someone from outside had crept in through the French windows and poisoned the tea things before we went into the dining room? Besides, he didn't eat anything, and the only thing he drank was that cup of tea. Since no one else is ill, it must just have been that cup that was poisoned, rather than the whole teapot—and that means that the murderer must have been in the room when he drank it. Everyone was crowding round the tea table—any of them could have dropped something into the cup before it was handed to him, couldn't they? They're all suspects, Daisy!"

I stopped and took a deep breath. It was an unusually long speech for me, and my stomach had been turning over as I said it. I was telling Daisy that any of her family might be a murderer, and I was terribly afraid that she was going to shout at me, or tell me that I was wrong. Even after more than a year of being friends, I never quite know how Daisy will take things.

"Golly!" she said, after a pause. "Yes. Remember Mr. Curtis saying that the tea tasted foul?"

"Exactly," I said, breathing a very quiet sigh of relief. "It's awful, but it must be true. So what do we do now?"

"Do? Why, Hazel, you chump, it's perfectly obvious. You may be all right at thinking, but you're absolutely no good at all at *doing*. You've just confirmed the scene of the crime, and we believe we've identified arsenic as the murder weapon. All the more reason for us to visit the dining room immediately and recover that cup—it will certainly still retain traces of arsenic, and it may even have the murderer's fingerprints on it."

I peered at her. "But the door's locked, Daisy!"

"I know *that*," said Daisy. "And I know Uncle Felix still has the key. But we don't have to use that one. There's a whole set hidden in the umbrella stand for when we want to break into the pantry after Mrs. D. has gone home for the night. Come on—all we need to do is fish out the ones in the stand and we'll be in that room in a trice."

Of course, Daisy is always right about this sort of thing, but as I stood up and followed her down the stairs I couldn't help worrying. We were starting off on our detective path, just as we had last year—and at the end of that path, once again, was a real murderer. What if they noticed that we were investigating, and came after us next? I remembered our last murder case, and shuddered. I never wanted to feel so frightened again. But of course, I couldn't say this to Daisy. The less safe Daisy is, the happier she is about it.

Down the little back stairs we crept—Daisy as daintily as the famous thief Raffles from the book, heel-toe, heel-toe, and me like a baby elephant—then across the second-floor landing, holding our breath, and down the main stairs.

We crept (and I stumbled), and at last we were down in the hall, the grandfather clock ticking like the beat of a heart. Fallingford is so full of *things* that walking through it at night is a dangerous activity—there are bits of furniture and stray carpets everywhere. The chests and dressers and things made horrible shadows across the walls, and whenever I saw them out of the corner of my eye my heart pounded. The suit of armor looked like a person in the dark, and I gasped before I could stop myself. But Daisy remained calm. She went toward the umbrella stand (an elephant's foot—a real one, all leathery and cracking: it gives me the horrors) while I stood nervously beside the dining room door. I pushed the handle, just to pass the time, and to my great surprise it gave, and the door swung open.

"Daisy!" I hissed. "Look! It isn't locked after all!"

Daisy turned, hand still outstretched toward the umbrella stand. "Goodness!" she said in surprise. "Uncle Felix *is* slipping. Well, that makes this far simpler for us."

It was just as we had left it—curtains open and tea things laid out. Dimly, I saw the remains of cakes and sandwiches, spilling crumbs all over the table. Cups were tilted over, and dark tea stains crept across the pale tablecloth. My stomach lurched, so that for a foolish moment I wondered if I had been poisoned too. Dying while having tea was such a horrible way to go—like being tricked by something that ought to be nice.

I picked up a scrap of paper that was sitting on the tablecloth and fiddled with it nervously. It was a bit of a printed page—at first I thought it was newspaper, but it was too thick and smooth under my fingers, like paper from a book. I peered at it, trying to make out words, but then Daisy seized my arm. I stuffed it into my pocket and turned to her.

"Hazel!" hissed Daisy, pointing to the chair where Mr. Curtis had been sitting. "Look!"

I squinted—and saw that the room was not quite as it had been after all. The tea might be all there, and the furniture might be pulled out the way it had been that afternoon—but there were two things missing. The teacup that Mr. Curtis had drunk from, and his gold watch. It was like one of Miss Alston's memory games, where you have to remember what has been moved. And nothing else had, I was sure of it.

"Might they have been moved by someone when Mr. Curtis was taken ill?" I asked doubtfully. But I knew that they had been next to Mr. Curtis's chair when Uncle Felix locked the door. And the more I thought about it, the more sure I was that Uncle Felix *had* locked the door.

Daisy shone her flashlight about the room in jumpy patterns—at the dining table, at the other chairs, at the sideboard—but the fat gold watch and the thin golden cup were nowhere to be seen.

"Daisy, if they're not here now . . ."

I did not even have to finish my sentence. It meant, of course, that since we had all been in the dining room, someone had come in and taken away Mr. Curtis's cup and watch—and *only* the cup and the watch. And that meant that our suspicions were absolutely right: Mr. Curtis really *had* been poisoned.

I took a deep, steadying breath.

And then something at the other end of the dining room rustled.

Robin Stevens

Other than Daisy's flashlight, there was only the wet half-light filtering through from outside to see by. Beyond its beam we could only make out shadows and shapes—and the dining room was long and crowded with tables and chairs.

"*Who's there?*" asked Daisy. She is exceedingly brave sometimes. I couldn't have spoken, even if I'd wanted to.

The room had gone very quiet, apart from the patter of the rain, but I could feel that someone—whoever it was—was crouching at the far end, not moving, not making a sound. I remembered the unlocked door, and cold rushed down my spine.

"*Who's there?*" hissed Daisy again.

The person pushed over a chair.

We screamed, and then we turned round and ran as though vicious dogs were snapping at our heels, out of the dining room and all the way up to the nursery. The stairs crunched and creaked as we did so, and I was terrified that someone would hear—but the pounding rain must have drowned out all noise.

Shaking, we crept back into the little nursery bathroom; it really was becoming our headquarters for this case, I thought. Daisy bolted the door, and we both sank down against it. For a while we were silent.

"I can't believe you screamed, Hazel," said Daisy at last. "You nearly gave the game away!"

I opened my mouth indignantly to point out how hypocritical she was being, and then closed it again. Daisy was just being Daisy, and did not mean it in the least.

"It was quite a *quiet* scream," I said. My voice came out all wobbly. "No one heard."

"Hazel," said Daisy, after another little while, "I think our case has just become *exceedingly* interesting. There is only one reason why someone who isn't us would be creeping about in the dining room in the dark, stealing the cup that Mr. Curtis was drinking from: because they murdered him, and they want to hide the evidence."

"But how did they unlock the door?" I asked. "Hardly anyone else knows about the keys in the umbrella stand, do they?"

"Daddy and Bertie do," said Daisy. "And anyone else might have crept into Uncle Felix's room while he was out of it and pinched the dining room key from his jacket pocket. The trouble is that they'll have put it back by now—either in the umbrella stand or by sliding the key under Uncle Felix's door—so we won't be able to discover anything that way."

"So they really do have to be from Fallingford House! And they know we're after them." I gulped. I was beginning to feel as though I had been sucked back into last autumn. It was all happening again: a hidden murder, and a murderer who knew that we were investigating the case.

"Well, that can't be avoided," said Daisy. "Sometimes detectives have to face terrible danger. Buck up, Hazel, and think about the important things. We're right about this being a case of murder!"

Something else occurred to me. "If they were there for the cup, why did they take the watch too?" I asked.

"Oh, exactly, Watson!" said Daisy. "That's an important line of investigation to follow. It's obvious why the murderer would take the cup—fingerprints and incriminating white residue, of course—but why would they take the watch? I—"

Someone rattled the doorknob. We both jumped to our feet in panic. My heart was in my mouth. How could the murderer have found us so soon?

"Squashy!" said Bertie's voice. "What are you doing in there again? Come out and stop being such an idiot. I need to, er . . ."

We were safe after all—but there was nothing for it: we crept out sheepishly to find Bertie standing there in his dressing gown, looking cross.

"Sorry," I said to him.

"Not sorry," said Daisy, sticking out her tongue.

Bertie made a horrible face, and swept past us into the bathroom.

We crept back to our beds again. I lay there, thinking. Why would the murderer steal the watch? Was it important somehow? Or was it simply valuable?

I remembered the way Aunt Saskia had looked at it the day before. Surely she wouldn't kill anyone for a watch, no matter how beautiful it was? But I couldn't be sure about anything. After all, someone in this house—perhaps even one of Daisy's family—must be the murderer.

It was becoming clear that this was a case where the truth might be even more awful than what we were imagining.

The next morning it was still raining; it poured and poured as though it would never stop. I knelt up on my bed and peered through the window bars at a countryside that was brown and heaving with water. It was as if, up on Fallingford's hill, we really were on a boat, sailing through a hostile ocean.

"Gosh," said Kitty, coming over and kneeling beside me. "At this rate we shan't be able to leave for *days*. Ugh. What if Mr. Curtis begins to rot?"

The thought of that made me feel ill. We were dealing with bodies again, and I know that, despite what Daisy's detective novels say, bodies are horrid things even when they are quite new. But the body, nasty though it was, was not the worst thing about being stuck at Fallingford. We knew now that we were trapped in a house *with a murderer*.

• • •

We had breakfast in the drawing room, as the dining room was still out of bounds. There was a mountain of food, as usual—toast and eggs and bacon and sausages—but the change of room made everything feel odd and wrong, and everyone was subdued. At least the food tasted the same.

Bertie chewed furiously through a mountain of toast, while Stephen only stared at his plate. Aunt Saskia hunched over and gulped down poached eggs without even glancing at the silver butter knife next to her plate, and Miss Alston cut a pear into smaller and smaller segments until it practically vanished. Uncle Felix bit into his napkin instead of his bacon, and seemed not to even notice. Lord Hastings only picked at his kedgeree, looking gray, and shifted about in his chair as though he were sitting on a spider. Chapman was behaving oddly too. He kept glancing at Lord Hastings, and then looking away again, as though desperate to say something but unable to get it out.

The rain was still lashing down against the windows, and the drawing room, which is always cold, looked unpleasant in the gray light. All attempts at conversation seemed to end up at death, like those houses you walk through in dreams where every door you open leads to the same nasty place.

At last Lord Hastings stared up at the ceiling and said, "Church this morning, of course."

"I shan't be going," said Lady Hastings tightly. Her eyes

were red and her hair was uncombed, and she had not even touched her bowl of bran. "I—I'm going to call the police."

Aunt Saskia dropped her fork.

"Mother!" said Bertie. "Why on earth . . . ?"

"Denis is dead!" cried Lady Hastings. "What do you mean, *why?*"

"I mean that police aren't generally interested in food poisoning!" said Bertie. "Honestly, Mother, that's not what they're for."

"Dr. Cooper doesn't think it was food poisoning," said Lady Hastings. "I heard him say so to Felix. And *Felix* doesn't think it was an accident."

At this bombshell, everyone froze.

"Margaret," said Uncle Felix sternly, "didn't I tell you that *I* would handle this?"

"Yes, you did, but I want the *proper* police," said Lady Hastings. I wondered again what exactly Uncle Felix *did* when he was not being Daisy's uncle. "Denis is *dead*, and after what I heard you say, I don't think I can trust anyone in this house, not even my own brother. I'm going to call up that lovely police officer who came to the house after . . . well, you know, after the *unfortunate thing* that happened at Daisy's school last year."

Beanie squealed, Daisy twitched, and I had to dig my fork into my leg to stop myself gasping. The Deepdean murder seemed to keep on coming up! The thought of seeing Inspector Priestley again, here, made me feel sick and excited, all at once. He had saved us once before—would he have to do it again?

"Ah yes," said Lord Hastings mournfully. "I knew that there would be a lovely police officer involved somehow."

"Oh, do be quiet," snapped Lady Hastings. "I'm calling him, and that's that. You can go to church and pretend to be sorry."

But there was to be no church for any of us. Chapman came over and whispered something in Lord Hastings's ear.

"The road to the village is flooded," said Lord Hastings, looking up and clearing his throat. "O'Brian had to be brought over by boat this morning, and now the cows in the long field are stranded. They need to be rescued. I shall go and supervise—but I'm afraid there's no chance of the boat being free before church."

"Well, in that case there's no point in calling the police," said Uncle Felix to Lady Hastings. "If Fallingford's flooded, all of Nussington Road's closed. They won't be able to get through."

"Which means we're trapped!" said Bertie. He sounded quite excited about it. "Trapped with a *dead body*."

Daisy's eyes lit up. Beanie burst into tears.

"Beans!" said Kitty. "Buck up, come on!"

"I—just—don't—like—death!" sobbed Beanie.

"Death!" said Lady Hastings. "It's not just death. It's

Robin Stevens

murder, and one of *you* did it!" In one graceful movement she threw down her handkerchief, pushed back her chair and rushed out of the room, sobbing.

Beanie clutched Kitty; she was white with fear. Even Kitty looked rather pale.

"This is nonsense," said Uncle Felix, standing up and screwing in his monocle. "The man had dysentery. That was what I was saying to Dr. Cooper. Margaret must have misunderstood me. We don't need the police."

I couldn't understand why Uncle Felix was pretending to be so ignorant. We had heard him tell Dr. Cooper his suspicions. That was how Daisy and I had been able to work out that it was poison in the first place. Was he just trying to make sure that everyone stayed calm? Or did he have another reason to lie?

Daisy turned a rather suspicious glare on him. "Dysentery?" she asked.

Uncle Felix stared back at her coolly, one eyebrow slightly raised, giving nothing away. It was an expression I have caught Daisy practicing in front of the mirror several times lately.

"Of course it was dysentery," he said. "What else would it be?"

As Daisy says, it is maddening being a child. We both wanted to stay down with the grown-ups to see what they would do next, but instead, straight after breakfast Miss Alston hustled us back up to the nursery. She seemed desperate to get rid of us—there was no talk of lessons later. In fact, she seemed quite distracted. As we climbed the stairs, she strode ahead, frumpy hair in a tangle and huge handbag over her arm. I studied her and wondered what was going through her head.

But Daisy had someone else on her mind.

"I can't believe Uncle Felix!" she muttered to me. "How dare he lie to *me*!"

Kitty turned to look at us, and her eyes narrowed. I immediately tried to look as ordinary as possible, so she would not suspect the detective things going on in my head; I thought I had been successful—until we got back to the nursery and the door closed behind us. Then Kitty pounced.

"You two are up to something," she said. "I can tell. It's something to do with Mr. Curtis, isn't it?"

"Why would you think that?" asked Daisy, deadpan. "We were only talking about what a fright Miss Alston looks, weren't we, Hazel?"

"Um," I said. "Yes."

"You were not!" said Kitty. "I'm not an idiot. You were talking about Mr. Curtis. You're playing your detective games again."

I have sometimes wondered whether the others knew, but it was still a shock to hear someone else talk about the Detective Society. It felt as though Kitty had kicked something sacred.

"I don't know what you mean!" said Daisy. "Detective games? Even if we were talking about Mr. Curtis—which we weren't—it wouldn't be a game, and you wouldn't be allowed to know about it."

"Oh, don't look so shocked—we've known about your society for ages, ever since what happened to Miss Bell last year. We all know—well, Beanie and I do. And we think it's utterly silly, otherwise we would have asked to join."

"Silly?" sputtered Daisy. "We solved a *murder*!"

Kitty sniffed. "The police did that," she said. "That handsome policeman your mother was talking about."

Daisy had gone pink. She was so furious that, for once, she was lost for words.

"So is it true, what your mother said at breakfast?" asked Kitty. "Has Mr. Curtis really been murdered?"

"No!" said Daisy, for once forgetting herself. "Go away, can't you? You'll spoil everything!"

"It *is* true!" cried Kitty triumphantly. "I knew it! Hah!"

Beanie's lip began to tremble.

"No!" I said desperately. "No, listen!"

"No, *you* listen," said Kitty. "If there's something that exciting happening at Fallingford, then we want in on it. It's not fair, you leaving us out. If you don't let us, we'll go to your uncle and tell him exactly what you're up to. And I bet he'll be furious."

"*You* might want to join in, but Beanie doesn't," said Daisy, grasping at straws. "Do you, Beanie? It's terribly dangerous. You might die!"

"You won't die!" I said to Beanie quickly. "But Daisy is right. It *is* dangerous."

Beanie took a deep breath. We could all see her considering.

"I think . . . ," she said at last. "I think that if you're going to be detectives, then I want to help. *Can't* I help?" Her eyes were wide, and she stared at Daisy like a kitten left out in the rain.

Daisy was silent. Then she sighed. "Bother," she said. "All *right*, then. But you're only temporary members of our society. You have to be our assistants."

Robin Stevens

"Assistants!" exclaimed Kitty, making a face.

"What's wrong with that? Sherlock Holmes had messengers, and that's a sort of assistant. Anyway, you can't just invite yourself into the Detective Society and expect to become important at once. Why, it took Hazel almost a whole semester to become vice president."

"Daisy!" I said. Like it or not, we had to be nice to Kitty and Beanie now that they were in on the secret.

"Oh, all right, if you prefer it, you can call yourselves *secret agents*. But you'll still be assistants, really."

This was the sort of Daisy compromise that was really no compromise at all.

Beanie squeaked again, with joy this time.

Daisy rolled her eyes. "Don't get too excited," she said. "If you're part of the Detective Society you have to solemnly agree to do whatever I tell you to, because I am the president. Hazel is the vice president and also the secretary, which means that she writes everything down and also helps me solve cases. Also, you have to swear yourselves to secrecy with the Detective Society pledge, which means that if you tell anyone about what we do, ever, we're allowed to hunt you down and punish you with medieval tortures."

"The medieval tortures part isn't true," I said quickly, because Beanie's eyes had grown almost bigger than her face.

"*Aren't* they!" said Daisy. "You're such a good vice president that I haven't needed to threaten you, but that doesn't mean they don't exist. In this case, though, I think the warning is needed. Kitty, Beanie, are you ready to swear? If you don't, you can't help us."

"I suppose," said Kitty, crossing her arms.

"All right," said Beanie. "I don't want to be tortured, please!"

"Good. Now, I'm going to say the pledge, and then at the end you have to say *I do*. Ready? Listen carefully.

"Do you swear to be a good and clever member of the Detective Society, and to logically detect the crimes presented to you using all the cleverness you have, not placing reliance on grown-ups, especially the police?"

She nudged Kitty, and Kitty jumped and said, "I do."

"I do," said Beanie, half a beat behind.

"Do you solemnly swear never to conceal a vital clue from your Detective Society president and vice president, and to do exactly what they say?"

"You're making this up now!" cried Kitty. "Oh, all right, I do."

"I do too!" said Beanie.

"Do you promise never to mention this to another soul, living or dead, on pain of medieval tortures?"

"I do," chorused Kitty and Beanie.

"Excellent," said Daisy, satisfied. "Now we can tell you about the case."

Robin Stevens

S o what have you discovered, then?" asked Kitty.

"Mr. Curtis *didn't* die of dysentery," said Daisy dramatically. "He *was* murdered."

"Well, we knew that," said Kitty. "Your mother said so."

"Yes, but we've proved it," said Daisy. I could tell that she was cross about Kitty's response—she hates to have her thunder stolen by anyone. "We overheard Uncle Felix talking about it to Dr. Cooper, and then we did some research to confirm it. Mr. Curtis was poisoned, at teatime—we have deduced that someone gave him arsenic from the rat poison tin in the hall cupboard."

"I don't see how you can have proof of any of that," said Kitty, who was turning out to be a not very obedient assistant. "You might just be imagining things."

"We are not!" said Daisy. "Just listen. We crept down to the dining room last night to look for Mr. Curtis's teacup—and someone had already got in and stolen it, and his watch as well! In fact, they nearly caught us. We had to be very quick."

"But why would anyone murder him?" asked Beanie. "Poor Mr. Curtis!"

"Lots of reasons!" said Daisy. "But the really important one is this: he was here to take our things. When he died, Hazel and I were already investigating him—we saw him creeping about, ogling all the nice things in the house and muttering about how valuable they were, and then he lied to Mummy and said that they were hardly worth anything at all. Then we saw . . . well, we saw something that made it clear he was trying to weasel his way into Mummy's affections, to trick her into selling him our things for a song."

"Oh, were they kissing?" asked Kitty. "I wondered."

I winced. "Lord Hastings, Uncle Felix, and Bertie knew what was going on between them too," I said quickly. "So they were all angry at Mr. Curtis. That's why everyone was so cross yesterday."

"Not the only reason," said Daisy, nodding, "but a very good one. Look, before we go any further, we might as well make this a formal meeting of the Detective Society. Hazel, you've got your casebook, haven't you? What have you called this case?"

"The Case of Mr. Curtis," I said, taking out the book.

"Very good," said Daisy. "Present at this meeting: Daisy Wells, president, and Hazel Wong, vice president and secretary. Also present, Katherine Freebody and Rebecca Martineau, assistants and temporary Detective Society members.

"Victim: Mr. Curtis. Cause of death: arsenic poisoning—although this can only be a very good guess, as we don't have access to the body—*again*! Honestly, why does this always seem to happen to us?

"Time of poisoning: teatime. It couldn't have been any earlier—the book Hazel and I read told us that arsenic usually only takes fifteen minutes or so to begin to work . . . Oh, just *think*, we really *saw* the murder happen!"

I shivered, and Beanie squeaked.

"And if there was any doubt, the missing teacup confirms it. The murderer knew that cup was important evidence, so they got rid of it."

"But who *is* the murderer?" asked Beanie fearfully.

"Good question!" said Daisy, beaming. "Because of the way that the murderer broke in to the dining room, Hazel and I have deduced that it must be someone in this house. Only one of us could have known about the spare keys in the umbrella stand, or have been able to slip into Uncle Felix's room to pinch the key that he had in his pocket."

Beanie looked terrified. I wanted to tell her that she would be all right—but I couldn't make myself say it when it might not be true. Had we done something awful by dragging her and Kitty into the investigation?

"We ought to make a list of suspects," I said instead. Lists, as I knew from our last murder case, made everything seem more safe. When it was all down in my casebook it became a puzzle, something we could manage, something more exciting than terrifying.

"So we ought!" said Daisy. "You know, I have some very good ideas about who it might be."

I looked at her. Her eyes were gleaming, and every bit of her was at attention and on the scent—just as though Mr. Curtis's death had happened in a faraway house, with quite different people. I thought of Uncle Felix, pretending to everyone that he didn't know Mr. Curtis had been poisoned. I thought of Aunt Saskia, begging Lady Hastings not to call the police, and I thought of Bertie, shouting so angrily at Lady Hastings and Mr. Curtis on Friday evening. Was Daisy really excited about suspecting one of her own family?

"Who?" I asked cautiously.

"Well, there is certainly one person who's been acting particularly suspiciously ever since Mr. Curtis arrived."

We all waited to hear what she would say.

Daisy sighed. "*Miss Alston*, of course," she said.

VIII

Kitty gasped. Of course, I knew what Daisy meant. Miss Alston had been odder than ever since Mr. Curtis arrived. I remembered the moment when she had emerged from the maze and he had spoken to her in that strange way, as though he knew something about her that we did not. And I remembered that bit of paper we had seen her stuffing into her handbag after breakfast yesterday. But all the same, I was concerned. I remembered what had happened the last time Daisy decided on a suspect so quickly.

"Are you *sure?*" I asked.

Daisy rolled her eyes. "*No,* I'm not sure," she said. "It's just a hypothesis. But you have to admit, it's a good one. We heard what Mr. Curtis said to her—he accused her of being at Fallingford for a reason other than being a governess, and I'm sure that's true. She's a very suspicious character—I'm certain she has a secret. It's extremely important that we watch her and try to discover what it is. Write her down on the list. Now, who else?"

I didn't want to be the first to mention someone from Daisy's family. I opened my mouth and shut it again. But then Kitty spoke.

"What about your aunt Saskia?" she asked. "You said that watch of Mr. Curtis's was missing with the teacup. Hasn't she been absolutely fixated on it all weekend? She might have murdered Mr. Curtis to get her hands on it. *And* she didn't want your mother to call the police."

Daisy blinked and frowned.

"I'm only *saying*," said Kitty, undaunted. "You asked who else might have done it."

"Yes," said Daisy. "You're quite right, of course. We know that the watch is missing, and we also know that Aunt Saskia is always taking things that don't belong to her. She's not a *thief*—people like *us* aren't—but she does . . . have a little problem. She's only ever taken small things that won't be missed, but I suppose that if she wanted the watch enough she might have done something silly to get it. Write that down too, Hazel."

"And what about Uncle Felix?" I put in, since the plunge had clearly been taken. "I know you like him, but you have to admit that he's been behaving strangely too. Why did he lie about Mr. Curtis being poisoned? We overheard him asking the doctor to take samples and send them to

London, so we know he thinks it's suspicious. And remember that conversation we overheard in the maze? He was telling Mr. Curtis that if he didn't leave, he'd do something awful. What if the murder was what he meant?"

"He wouldn't!" said Daisy heatedly. "He . . . You don't know Uncle Felix!"

"Because you won't tell us about him!" I said. "*Are* those rumors about him true?"

Daisy flushed. "I shan't tell you," she said at last. I had a feeling she really meant, *I don't know.* "But he—oh, all right. You can put him down on your list for now. But I'll rule him out—you'll see!"

IX

At that moment the door opened and Bertie came in, with Stephen just behind him. Bertie was tinkling away at his ukulele again. It had gone flat in the damp, and was letting out sour, off-tune notes. Bertie looked just as angry as he always did, and I wondered about *him* as a suspect. He did get into such horrible rages—and he knew about Mr. Curtis and Lady Hastings.

Daisy wrinkled up her nose at him. "Go away," she said. "We're busy. What are you *playing*, anyway?"

"The 'Funeral March,'" said Bertie, strumming obnoxiously. "And I might ask the same thing of you, Squashy. What are *you* all playing at?"

Daisy glared. "A game," she said. "You wouldn't be interested."

Bertie narrowed his eyes—looking, as he did so, exactly like Daisy sometimes does. I couldn't decide whether it was funny or creepy. "I know all your secrets, Squashy," he said. "I'm only lucky that you don't know all mine."

"Why?" snapped Daisy. "What have you done now?"

"Well, despite what Mother says, I didn't kill Mr. Curtis," said Bertie. "In fact, I don't believe anyone did. Do you, Stephen?"

Stephen went pale. "I don't know," he said. I could tell that he hated the discussion. I felt quite sorry for him.

"You see?" said Bertie. "He thinks it's a stupid question. Honestly, how did Mother get that idea in her head? I know she's a bit silly sometimes, but this is something else!"

"Mummy can be an idiot," said Daisy. "I expect she simply misheard Dr. Cooper."

Bertie snorted, and even Stephen grinned.

"Now go away," Daisy repeated, "or we'll make you play dolls with us."

"Horror!" said Bertie, and he made the ukulele jangle in pain.

I caught Stephen's eye. His freckles were standing out more than ever, but he gave me a smile, and I felt better at once. Stephen was bearing up, and I could too.

"All right," said Daisy, when they had gone. "Thank goodness we don't really have to play dolls. Back to our suspect list. Who else can we put down? I know who we can rule out. If we're saying that the poison must have been given to Mr. Curtis at tea, it means that the murderer must have been in the dining room itself when tea was served, to drop the poison into his teacup—it can't have been in the pot, after all. Hetty and Mrs. Doherty weren't there, so they can be ruled out at once—I'm glad about that. Oh, and I say! Don't you remember how far Mummy made Chapman stand from the tea table? He never went near it. He couldn't have doctored Mr. Curtis's cup—he's out too!"

I had suddenly thought of something. "How do you think the murderer got the poison into the cup from the tin?" I asked.

"Perhaps they wrapped it up in their handkerchief, or a bit of paper. I've read about that in a book," said Daisy. "Then they tipped it into Mr. Curtis's cup when no one was looking."

I put my hand in my pocket and pulled out the paper I had found on the dining room table the night before.

"A bit of paper like this?" I asked. "I found it in the dining room last night, but I didn't think . . . I forgot, with all the excitement about the cup."

"Hazel!" Daisy gasped. "You clever thing! A clue, a real clue!"

All four of us bent over it. It really *was* half a page from a book, the words close-printed. There was a little smear of pale powder on one edge—and when I saw that, I knew that there could be no doubt. This *was* what the murderer had used to keep the poison in.

When I realized that, I was quite horrified. What if I had been poisoned, keeping it in my pocket like that?

"Don't worry," said Daisy. "There isn't enough there

anymore to kill anything bigger than a mouse. You're quite safe, Hazel. Just—ask Mrs. D. to wash your clothes quite carefully, next time?"

Comforted, I took a breath, and we all read the text:

struck again,
And growing still in stature the grim shape
For so it seemed, with purpose of its own
And measured motion like a living thing,
Strode after me. With trembling

"Ugh, rubbishy poetry," said Daisy. "I don't blame the murderer for tearing it up. But this evidence is still very good! We must be on the lookout for the book this came from. It's an important step forward with the investigation. All right, let's continue with our suspects. Who else is there?"

"Lord Hastings," I said, because someone had to. "He knew about . . . your mother and Mr. Curtis. He might have wanted to take revenge. After all, we saw him get cross at Mr. Curtis yesterday morning."

"We saw him tell Mr. Curtis to leave!" said Daisy. "And he knew that Mr. Curtis was going to the station yesterday. Why would he kill him after that?"

"But, Daisy," I said. "He did shout at him. We all heard."

"Yes, yes, I do admit that we can't rule him out," she said sharply. "He was at the tea table at the right time, and he did have a reason to hate Mr. Curtis. All right, put him down *for the moment*.

"Oh, and I know!" she added, dropping Lord Hastings out of the discussion as if he was a hot coal in her hand. "What about Bertie? We must add him to the list—it'll make him fearfully cross. He does get so angry sometimes, I wouldn't be surprised if he was secretly a homicidal maniac. Can't you imagine him bumping off Mr. Curtis?"

"Do you really believe that?" asked Beanie.

"Of course I don't," said Daisy. "He's my *brother*. But we're adding everyone to the list, aren't we? We might as well suspect them all, while we're at it. So Daddy, Bertie . . . Who else? Oh yes, Stephen."

"What motive does he have?" I could feel my cheeks going pink. "He doesn't know Mr. Curtis, does he, and he can't be angry about Lady Hastings."

"Ooh-ooh," said Kitty. "Hazel's fond of Stephen!"

Daisy looked at me, and my face heated up even more. I couldn't help it.

"Bertie's told me a bit about Stephen's past," she said. "His father's gone, and his mother's terribly poor. What if he killed Mr. Curtis to steal the watch and sell it?"

"How tragic!" said Kitty gleefully.

"Poor Stephen!" said Beanie.

"I'd say the money angle's not a bad one. Write it down, Hazel."

I did—and then I said, "One person left. What about Lady Hastings?"

It was quite cruel of me, I know, but after what Daisy had just said, I wanted to jab at her.

"But I thought you said that she liked Mr. Curtis?" Beanie asked shyly. "Why would she kill someone she liked?"

"But we—I—saw her arguing with Mr. Curtis yesterday afternoon," I said, reluctant to tell Daisy what I'd seen, but knowing that I had no choice now. "He wanted her to run away with him, and bring her jewels and a painting, and she wouldn't, and Mr. Curtis was angry. He said he was going to tell Lord Hastings—what if she killed him to stop him doing that?"

Daisy frowned. "You ought to have told me at once!" she said. "That's important information! But all the same, Mummy isn't really clever enough to plan something like dropping poison in a cup—I'm sure that if she tried, someone would notice immediately. However, what you saw means that we can't rule her out yet. She can go down on the list for the moment."

SUSPECT LIST

Miss Alston. MOTIVE: Unknown. But we suspect that she has some sort of secret history which Mr. Curtis knew about. OPPORTUNITY: Was at the tea table at the crucial time. Could have stolen the poison from the hall. NOTES: Was seen being threatened by Mr. Curtis outside the maze by Daisy Wells and Hazel Wong. Was seen hiding a piece of paper suspiciously. Who is she really, and what is she doing here? We must investigate.

Aunt Saskia. MOTIVE: Wanted Mr. Curtis's watch. OPPORTUNITY: Was at the tea table at the crucial time. Could have stolen the poison from the hall. NOTES: Has been behaving suspiciously. Does not want the police to get involved–although this could be because of other misdemeanours in her past. Search her room for the watch?

Uncle Felix. MOTIVE: Rage at Mr. Curtis over Lady Hastings. He was heard in the maze threatening Mr. Curtis by Daisy Wells and Hazel Wong. OPPORTUNITY: Was at the tea table at the crucial time. Could have stolen the poison from the hall. NOTES: We know he has lied about Mr. Curtis's cause of death. Why?

Lord Hastings. MOTIVE: Jealousy. OPPORTUNITY: Was at the tea table at the crucial time. Could have stolen the poison from the hall. NOTES: Seen shouting at Mr. Curtis on Saturday morning and telling him to leave Fallingford.

Robin Stevens

Bertie Wells. MOTIVE: Rage at Mr. Curtis over Lady Hastings. OPPORTUNITY: Was at the tea table at the crucial time. Could have stolen the poison from the hall.

Stephen Bampton. MOTIVE: He is not well-off. Could he have stolen Mr. Curtis's watch to sell it? OPPORTUNITY: Was at the tea table at the crucial time. Could have stolen the poison from the hall.

Lady Hastings. MOTIVE: Mr. Curtis threatened her. She might have killed him to stop him carrying out his threat. OPPORTUNITY: Was at the tea table at the crucial time. Could have stolen the poison from the hall.

"All right," said Daisy, "I think that wraps up the meeting."

"So what are we going to do now?" Beanie asked.

"Gather evidence, of course. We need to investigate each of our suspects. For example, we must see if we can uncover something about Miss Alston's past. Can we discover her letter of reference? She must have one. We could look in her room—perhaps she keeps her papers there. Then there's the piece of paper Hazel found, with the poison on it. Which book did it come from? And we ought to conduct interviews with Chapman, Mrs. Doherty, and Hetty. We know they didn't do it, but servants' evidence is usually the most crucial. As detectives, we'd be fools to leave them out. With any luck we'll be able to wrap up the case before the police arrive."

I felt the same old detective excitement rising up in me. Daisy was getting to me, turning real things into puzzles to be solved—but then I wondered whether it wasn't better to think of Mr. Curtis as a puzzle than as a real person who had been *murdered*. When I thought about that I felt full-up with awfulness, not excited at all.

"Where do we start?" asked Kitty. Detective fever seemed to have infected her too—her eyes were shining as she shook her hair back from her forehead.

"Miss Alston's bedroom," said Daisy, "since she's downstairs with the other grown-ups. At the moment she seems the most likely culprit, but we need to learn more about her. We can look for that paper she was hiding, *and* the teacup and watch into the bargain."

We crept out onto the landing. It was empty. My heart was beating fast—I couldn't quite believe that we were about to break in to Miss Alston's little room. What if she came up and found us?

The door was shut. Daisy went tiptoeing up to it, twisted the handle, and carefully pushed it open.

It felt most dreadfully wrong. Miss Alston was such a secretive person—we really knew nothing about her at all. I had never even seen inside her bedroom, and neither had any of the others. I imagined her doorway as an invisible line that, if crossed, would burn you up into a crisp or freeze you to death.

"Oh no!" whispered Beanie as Daisy poked a careful shoe tip through the doorway, then craned her neck round, and I could tell that she felt as uncomfortable as I did.

"What is it, Beanie?" said Daisy, without turning her head.

"I don't think this is legal!" whispered Beanie nervously.

"Of *course* it's not legal, Beanie. But we're detecting, so that makes things all right."

"I don't want to go in!" Beanie's face crumpled.

"All right, then, stay out here! No one's making you. You can be our lookout. If Miss Alston comes up the stairs, whistle, or squeak, or something. Hazel, Kitty, are you coming?"

With Beanie trembling on the landing, we had to. Shooting nervous glances at each other, Kitty and I crept forward, and over the dividing line into Miss Alston's bedroom. I did not burn up—although I did feel a rush of shame that made me tingle with heat all the way to the tips of my fingers.

Inside, everything was neatly ordered—drawers shut, bed made with military precision, and a gleaming row of schoolbooks laid out in alphabetical order. It was so neat that I was terrified all over again. What if we left signs of our presence? If she was not the murderer, she would be furious. And if she *was* . . . I shivered.

But Daisy seemed to have no concerns at all.

"Oh, do come along," she hissed at us, tugging a drawer of Miss Alston's bureau open. "We'll never solve the mystery if you're so weak about it. Hmph—only combies."

"Daisy!" I cried, half shocked at what she was doing and half shocked at the sight of Miss Alston's white combinations.

"Come on, hurry up about it," said Daisy. "We must search! Paper, watch, cup—remember? Quickly!"

But although Daisy raked through the contents of the

Robin Stevens

bureau, sending dull brown skirts and sweaters spinning into the air like birds bursting out of the undergrowth on an English walk, her search yielded no results.

"Nothing here," she groaned. "Come on, Hazel, hurry up! Kitty, be useful and fold these clothes."

I did look. Really I did. I looked inside each of Miss Alston's books, wafts of new-book smell ruffling my hair as I did so, and I even pulled her shiny brown suitcase out from under the bed and ran my fingers across the lining. That's where people keep stolen jewels in stories, after all. But there was nothing. No watch, no cup, no letter of reference and nothing that could have been the paper we had seen her hide. In fact, no letters of any kind. And although we had been through Miss Alston's room quite thoroughly, we hadn't found a single personal item. No family photographs, no notes from friends. She was as mysterious as ever.

"She really is an awfully private person," I said to Daisy. "Do you think she even *has* a family? There aren't any snapshots of them."

Daisy sat back on her heels. "She *must* have a family," she said. "Everyone does . . . unless—wait, Hazel, wait! You might have a point!"

Kitty and I waited.

"Look at this room," said Daisy. "Look at the things in it. You ought to be able to tell about someone from their surroundings. What does this tell us? Nothing. The books are new, and there aren't even any inscriptions in them. The clothes are brand-new too—they don't even look as if they have been washed. She might have bought new outer things for this visit, but surely she's not rich enough to have bought new underwear. And yet it's all new! Even her case is new. Just look at it! No customs labels, no scratches on the leather. What's wrong is that nothing's wrong. It's all too perfect! These aren't possessions; they're *props*."

"What does that mean?" I asked. I realized that Daisy was quite right. This whole room was a gap where a personality ought to be. Miss Alston was not a real person at all.

"It means," said Daisy, "that even though we haven't found any real clues, we are closer to understanding Miss Alston's secret. Whatever she is, we know what she isn't: she isn't a real governess; she is merely playing the part of one. We need to know what she's shown Mummy and Daddy, and how she managed to get herself here, teaching us. What Hazel and I heard yesterday proves that Mr. Curtis knew something about her that she didn't want to come out—we must discover what that was."

"*How?*" asked Kitty. "If you ask her, I doubt she'll tell you anything."

Daisy rolled her eyes. "Of course I'm not going to ask *her*," she said. "I'm not going to ask anyone. I'm going to find the letter she sent Mummy and Daddy when she applied for the post of governess."

Robin Stevens

B eanie was still standing outside on the landing, her face more pinched and worried than ever.

"Excellent guarding, Beans," said Kitty.

"Yes, good stuff," added Daisy, not really looking at her. "Now, can we get on?"

"Daisy," said Beanie, in a very small voice.

"Our search was inconclusive," said Daisy. "We're off to Daddy's study to see if we can find anything more helpful."

"Daisy," said Beanie again.

"What is it, Beanie? You're not still worried that we did something wrong, are you?"

"Not exactly," said Beanie, in the tiniest voice imaginable. "It's just that . . . I think I found something."

Beanie unclasped her hands from behind her back and brought them round where we could see. Clutched in them was a small black notebook. "I was standing waiting for you," she said, "and I was looking around, in case someone came up behind me and surprised me, and then I suddenly looked down and saw this. It was just by the top of the stairs, and I nearly didn't see it because it's so dark, and the banisters are dark too. I think someone must have dropped it."

"What is it?" asked Daisy, ready to shrug it off.

"Oh, I haven't looked yet," said Beanie. "I was afraid to."

Daisy sighed and snatched the book out of her hands. "It's probably just Chapman's to-do list," she said. "Or Miss Alston's lesson planner. I'm sure—"

But then her eyes went wide, and wider, and her mouth opened in a gasp of excitement.

"What is it?" asked Kitty. "Ugh. It looks dirty."

I had to admit that it did rather. It was all bent and fraying, and the black leather had gone gray at the edges.

"Hazel, come look at this and tell me whether I'm going quite insane," said Daisy softly, without looking up.

Kitty and Beanie stared at me jealously as I took the book, and opened it. *Property of Denis Curtis*, it said on the first page, and all the other pages were squeezed full of rows and rows of words, all squashed together in the most minute black lettering. It was a long, long list of names, with tiny notes next to each.

Henry. Visited house 16.8.1932: Meissen tea set—had no idea of worth. Offered to take it off his hands for £10. 18.8.1932: sold for £130.

Robin Stevens

Abbot. Visited house 2.10.1932: necklace, diamonds and rubies. Took straight off the neck of his lovely wife. Suggested it must have fallen into a pot in the conservatory. We hunted, no joy. 5.10.1932: sold for £800.

Schultz. 28.1.1933: old master in a drawer. Liberated it into my suit-case. Sold for £460.

I flicked forward through the book, past pages and pages of little names. *Ferrars, Lord Digby-Jones, Mackintosh, Petrey (MP)*—half the important people in the country seemed to be here, and their valuables. I turned to the final pages, a little spark of horror going through me, and saw:

Wells ('Lord Hastings'). Visited house 12.4.1935: Ming vase—but too large to lift! Chippendale furniture, and some very good paintings too. Old master in the downstairs hallway! May have some luck with jewels. Lovely wife responsive, has no idea of value of anything. Should be easy money!

"Daisy," I said. "It's the notebook we saw Mr. Curtis with yesterday! We were *right*."

"HA!" cried Daisy. "Yes! We said it all along! Mr. Curtis was a criminal, and now we have proof!"

"But—" Kitty started.

"There's no doubt, Kitty. You look at this book and tell

me that it's not a list of all of Mr. Curtis's dastardly thieving. *Tell* me!"

She thrust it in Kitty's face, and Kitty flicked through it, frowning.

"Well . . . ," she said. "Well—all right, it is."

Beanie gasped. "But why would he put his name on it?" she asked.

"If I'd done bad things, I wouldn't write it down in a book at all," said Kitty.

"I'd write it in code," I said.

"Well, I know *you* would," said Daisy to me. "That's because you're clever. Mr. Curtis was stupid and vain, and so it absolutely fits that he'd do something so—so *smug!*"

"Are you going to show anyone?" asked Beanie.

Daisy paused. "No," she said. "I think I'll wait until we have more evidence. Until we can announce who the murderer is as well."

Daisy had told Uncle Felix about her suspicions so eagerly a few days before. Everything had changed since then. We could no longer be sure that he was on our side. We could not even be sure that he was not the guilty person.

Daisy flicked through the little notebook again, and she scowled. "Bother!" she said. "It's all in date order, rather than alphabetical, and it's written so small! How are we ever to know if any of our suspects are in here? Hazel, you'll have to read it."

Just then, we heard loud voices below us. They came from somewhere deep down in the house, and they sounded very cross indeed. Reading the notebook would have to wait. Daisy and I glanced at each other, and then she motioned us all downstairs.

We crept down the front stairs together. I felt most dreadfully nervous, and as always when we go on detective missions, quite sure that anyone who saw us would know what we were up to at once. The notebook felt very hot and guilty in the pocket of my skirt—but as usual, I need not have worried. When we reached the hall we found everyone much too busy to bother wondering about us.

Lady Hastings, Aunt Saskia, and Uncle Felix were standing there, and they were all shouting at each other.

"I *tell* you, Margaret, I have everything under control!" said Uncle Felix. His cheeks were flushed and his monocle was dangling down from his jacket pocket, swinging with every gesture he made. "Mr. Curtis's room and the dining room are locked. Dr. Cooper has taken samples, and he will send them to London as soon as the roads open again. Even if they could get here—which they certainly cannot with the floods so high— there is simply nothing else the police could do."

"They could interview us," said Lady Hastings. "They could *believe* me. I still don't think you do, Felix!"

"You *mustn't* call the police, Margaret!" said Aunt Saskia urgently. She was squeezing her fingers in her fur stole, and bits of her hair were escaping from their pins down around her shoulders. She was only wearing one earring, and her stole glared at me with its beady little button eyes. "I mean to say—it's not nice. People like us don't call the police. We can sort this out on our own, can't we?"

"*Doesn't she look a fright?*" Kitty muttered in my ear.

"Good Lord, this is maddening!" said Lady Hastings. "What is wrong with you all? Anyone would think you weren't sorry that Mr. Curtis was dead! Well, I'm calling the police this minute, and there's not a thing any of you can say to stop me!"

She pounced on the telephone.

"The line will still be down from last night," said Uncle Felix—but it wasn't. I saw a flicker of annoyance chase across his face.

"Operator!" cried Lady Hastings. "I want the Deepdean Police. Immediately."

Aunt Saskia pulled her fur stole around her. Uncle Felix paced, fists clenched in his pockets. We four glanced at each other. I could tell that Kitty, especially, was adoring the scene.

"Hello!" said Lady Hastings. "Hello! . . . This is Lady Hastings, and I want to report a murder. Hello? What . . . ? No, I am not making it up . . . Don't be ridiculous! Of course I am. I am Lady Hastings, of Fallingford House, and one of my houseguests has been murdered."

"This is just like the pictures!" whispered Kitty in excitement.

"I say, *will* you pass me to Inspector Priestley? I know him— Listen to me—one of my guests has been murdered and if you do not pass this telephone to your inspector *immediately* I shall have you fired . . . Hello? I say, hello . . . ? Oh, Inspector Priestley, there you are . . . Yes, this is she . . . Yes, really murdered . . . Yes, Fallingford House . . . How? Poison. Yesterday. It was simply awful. You must come at once . . . Yes, we're fearfully flooded . . . What? Don't you have boats . . . ? Well, come as soon as you can, then. I tell you, a man has been poisoned! Good-bye."

She slammed down the receiver and turned to look at us all. "There," she said. "That's done. Now, if you'll excuse me, I need to be by myself in the library."

"I'm leaving," said Aunt Saskia. "At once. I can't bear—"

"As you know perfectly well, we are all trapped here," said Uncle Felix.

Aunt Saskia made a gasping, choking noise, and fled past us up the stairs, shedding a scarf and a jangling bracelet as she went. The bracelet nearly hit Beanie.

"Oh dear!" whispered Beanie. "Do you think Daddy will still be able to come for us tomorrow?"

"Now," said Uncle Felix, turning to us. It gave me a little jolt of shock. I was realizing that he was just as noticing a person as Daisy. "What are you four up to? Listening in, were you?"

"No," said Daisy coolly. "We were on our way down to see Daddy, and you stopped us. We couldn't very well creep past while you were all shouting at each other, could we?"

"Hmm," said Uncle Felix. "As usual, a likely story."

"You haven't *really* locked Mr. Curtis's room too?" asked Daisy.

"Indeed I have," said Uncle Felix, staring down at her through his monocle. "We don't want to end up with a body that has been picked over by small girls."

"I'm fourteen!"

"Regardless. Sometimes, Daisy, you need to learn to leave well alone. This is for people who know what they're doing."

I could see how much that hurt Daisy. She took a step back, mouth open. "The police, you mean?" she asked when she had got her breath back. "Why don't you want Inspector Priestley to come? You do think something odd's going on, I know you do! We heard you last night—"

"*What* did you hear last night?" Uncle Felix's voice had gone all silky, just the way it had been in the maze the day before. I stepped away from him in alarm, and even Daisy shrank back a little.

"Nothing," she said, bluffing it out. "Nothing at all."

"Run along, Daisy," said Uncle Felix. "Run along. If you are really looking for him, I believe your father's study is that way."

"You know perfectly well it is," said Daisy. "All right. We're running."

When we got to the study, Lord Hastings was alone; he was sitting in a worn leather armchair facing the fire, his slippered feet propped up on Toast Dog, who was curled up in a fat snoring ball. Millie was draped across his lap like a rug. There were paintings and knickknacks of all sorts—feathers and bits of paper—hanging on the walls.

At first I was glad that Miss Alston wasn't there, considering our purpose, but the more I thought about it, the odder it seemed. If Miss Alston was not with us, and not with Lord Hastings, where was she? She was supposed to have a job to do—what was she here for, after all?

"Hello, Daughter, Daughter's friends," said Lord Hastings in a slightly mournful voice. "What can I do for you?"

"We're bored," said Daisy. "It's raining. We thought we'd come and say hello." Then she turned to me and, quiet as a breath, said, "Desk. Look for Alston's papers. Quick. I'll distract him." Then she pushed Millie aside and perched herself on the arm of her father's chair.

"Daddy," she said, "what shall we do? And don't say 'Teach Toast Dog circus tricks,' the way you did last time. I know perfectly well that won't work, and besides, I'm not eight."

"Let's see," said Lord Hastings. "Are you too old for treasure hunts?"

"All but the very good ones." Daisy turned and widened her eyes at me. Using Kitty and Beanie as a shield, I crept toward Lord Hastings's desk. It was simply littered with papers—piles and piles of them. I had no idea how I would ever find a particular one. I began to shift through them, as carefully as I could. Receipts, land deeds, family trees—it seemed as if every paper the Wells family owned was here. Kitty and Beanie hovered in front of me, Beanie chewing at her braid and wriggling with nerves. I was quite sure that my search would come to nothing. Lord Hastings was looking away, at Daisy, but surely he would notice what I was doing before long? Then I heard Daisy.

"I do admit that Miss Alston is quite good at treasure hunts, but her lessons are terribly boring," she said. Daisy can be an excellent liar when she wants to be. "She's such a dull old thing! Really, whereever did you find her?"

"Odd story, that," said Lord Hastings, shifting his feet on Toast Dog, who grumbled in his sleep. "She wrote to us.

Said she'd heard we were looking. But she came from an agency—the . . . Oh, it began with an H, or an R—and she had all her references."

"In March?" asked Daisy.

"No, it began with an R, Daisy, not an M—oh, I see. Yes, March or thereabouts. It was terribly convenient. We hadn't even got round to advertising."

"So *not long ago*," said Daisy. "It can't be *too* far down. I'm sure if you think logically, you'll remember." Her voice had become louder for a moment, and I knew she was giving me a message. I looked at the papers again. If they went by date—newest on the top—then all I had to do was find March 1935. There was April. I shifted papers again, barely breathing. A bill from Liberty's. Another from the grocer. A plan of a field. And a letter with an official-looking letterhead that said: THE REPUTABLE AGENCY.

IS March 1935

Dear Lord Hastings,

I write to you to offer my services . . .

It was clipped to two other pieces of paper, and quick as a flash I scooped up all three and jammed them under my cardigan. Beanie squeaked. Kitty looked at me, and then over at Daisy and Lord Hastings, and said, "You know, Daisy, I think I've got an idea for a game after all. We all get a bit of paper—it's called Found."

Next to her, Beanie opened her mouth to protest—but then she understood. Her eyes bulged out of her head with excitement, and she squeezed her hands together.

"I don't think I've heard of that," said Lord Hastings. "Is it new?"

"The absolutely newest!" said Daisy, beaming. "Kitty, you are a brick for thinking of it. Come on, everyone, off we go! Thank you, Daddy, you've been tremendously interesting to talk to. You've inspired us."

"Delighted, Daughter dear," said her father. "Be a good girl, now."

"Always," said Daisy in her most innocent voice, shooing me out of the door as quickly as she could. I breathed in and tried not to crackle.

XIV

T he drawing room was empty, so we all rushed in, and
Daisy closed the door and leaned on it. I breathed
in again and the letters fell out from under my cardigan onto the carpet.

"Ooh, what do they say?" asked Beanie breathlessly.

We spread them out, and read.

15 March 1935

Dear Lord Hastings,

I write to you to offer my services as governess to
your daughter, the Honorable Daisy Wells. I have become
aware that the position is vacant, and I believe
that I am ideally qualified to impart knowledge to
Miss Wells. I am newly registered with the Reputable
Agency, but have worked as a governess in some of

the most respectable households in the land for many years, and can provide impressive references (attached). Please write to me at the PO Box indicated with your response—I am available immediately.

Yours sincerely,

Lucy Alston (Miss)

"Oh," said Kitty, disappointed. "So she really is a governess."

"What do you mean?" asked Daisy. "This letter practically *confirms* that Miss Alston lied to Mummy and Daddy. First of all, whatever is the Reputable Agency? Reputable *what*? It's far too vague to be a real thing. Second, she as good as tells us that she's only just joined it—so what agency was she with before, and why did she leave, if she's so qualified and excellent? Third, how did she find out that the position was open? She doesn't say at all, and Daddy told us he didn't advertise. And fourth, she's far too eager. *Available immediately?* That's deeply suspicious. Now to look at her references."

There were two, one written on thick cream paper with a gold letterhead, and one typed, rather badly, on paper with a heavy bluish grain. The first was from Lady Eveleigh, and the second from Professor Roger Fox-Trottenham. Both were utterly glowing about Miss Alston's qualifications and

Robin Stevens

teaching ability. *I would advice you to take her on without delay,* wrote Lady Eveleigh. *I was adviced by my good friend Lord Dutton to hire Miss Alston, and I have not regretted it for an instant,* wrote Professor Fox-Trottenham.

"Daisy!" I said, confused. "Look, they both—"

"They both use the wrong sort of *advise!*" hissed Daisy. "And look at their signatures!"

They looked quite different at first—but then I saw it. The G of *Roger* and the G of *Eveleigh* had the same thick loop with a flick at the end.

I sat back on my heels.

"I think," said Daisy, going pink with excitement, "that these two letters were written by *the same person!*"

"Golly!" said Kitty. I could tell that, in spite of herself, she was impressed. Beanie's eyes had gone rounder than ever.

Miss Alston's references were fakes. She was lying, and she was here because of a lie. But why? What did she want with Fallingford? And how were we to find out?

"What shall we do?" Beanie said exactly what I was thinking. I was stumped—but, of course, nothing ever halts Daisy's mind for long. If she comes up against a problem, she bounds round it and keeps on chasing after the truth. She stared at the three of us, beaming.

"It's perfectly obvious!" she said. "We're going to speak to the only other people who have any idea what goes on in this house. Mrs. Doherty and Hetty."

XV

We managed to creep out of the drawing room and across the hall to the kitchens without seeing anyone. The kitchens are lovely. I am quite sure that nothing has changed in them since Queen Victoria was alive—all cold stone and shiny brass, with great wooden racks swinging up above your head, which are quite alarming until you realize that they are only for drying things. Mrs. Doherty the cook, though, makes the place feel warm and full of food—there are always broken bits of a tart that did not quite turn out as expected, and cooling trays of biscuits where one or two have burned on their undersides and need to be eaten up. Mrs. Doherty is very little and smiling, with clipped gray hair under her white cap, and she moves very fast, as though there is never enough time in the day.

When we came in she was standing among Lord Hastings's bright but fading flowers, peeling carrots, her knife flashing and sparks of orange flying out into the air all around her; Hetty had her red hair tied back under her cap and her thin hands buried in the sink, washing up.

Daisy cleared her throat and they both looked up.

"Hello, Miss Daisy, love," said Mrs. Doherty. "Come for your bunbreak? If you're hungry there's a treacle tart with a burned side that can't go out at lunch, and macaroons too. I made them yesterday, but I forgot to put them out at tea."

My heart jumped at the mention of yesterday's birthday tea—but all the same I couldn't stop my mouth watering. The macaroons were piled up on a plate, all fat and golden and tempting.

"Golly," said Daisy. "You are a brick, Mrs. D. Can I have both?"

"Of course you can," said Mrs. Doherty, beaming, "as it's you."

"And you lot can have the same," said Daisy to the three of us, "as you're with me."

The macaroons were heavenly, like biting into a puff of coconut, and the tart was rich and sticky. I chewed happily (one bite of one, and then one of the other, to keep on surprising my mouth) and listened to Daisy talk.

"Isn't it funny about Miss Alston?" said Daisy conversationally, biting a perfect circle around the edge of her macaroon. "How she came here, I mean. Daddy told me that she applied out of the blue, just like that! Imagine! She must have heard about my genius."

Mrs. Doherty laughed. "Your genius, eh?" she said, giving Hetty a wink.

Hetty grinned back, gave a side plate one final swoop with her cloth and set it down on the side. "Yes, you're famous as anything," she said. "You ought to watch out, you'll have the king here for you next."

I smiled to myself. There is a part of Daisy that *does* think that, one day, she will have the king congratulating her.

"Mind you, Miss Alston is a bit odd," Hetty went on. "Mrs. D. and I were talking about it only the other day. Keeps herself to herself—not even any personal bits in her room! She must keep everything in that handbag of hers, but she *never* puts it down."

"Really?" asked Daisy. Beanie choked on her tart.

"*And* all her clothes are new. I think she's a princess in disguise, and Mrs. D. thinks she's a spy."

"That was a joke," said Mrs. Doherty, beginning to peel again without looking down at what her hands were doing. "But she is a funny one. When I tried to speak to her about Mr. Curtis, she shut up like a clam."

"She's been even more odd since . . . what happened," said Hetty, glancing at Kitty and Beanie. "She keeps popping up everywhere I go. I'd think I was imagining it, but Mrs. D's noticed it too."

"This weekend!" said Mrs. Doherty. "Miss A. lurking about all over the house, your aunt making the teaspoons

Robin Stevens

go missing, your brother playing that dreadful instrument at all hours, and that poor sweet penniless friend of his, with no good clothes to his name—Hetty's been darning his socks in secret. And now a dead body in one of the guest rooms! Hetty can't get in to clean. Infuriating. Your uncle won't even let us into the dining room to clear the tea. I can only imagine what nasty things are happening to all those cakes, left without a covering. We shall have more rats than ever."

Kitty was listening with eyes wide and mouth in a greedy O. This was a perfect heaven of gossip for her.

"How do you know Stephen hasn't any money?" asked Daisy.

I shifted uncomfortably. I wished she would leave Stephen alone.

"I found his wallet in the hall yesterday," said Hetty. "Of course, I had to open it to know whose it was. All I found inside was tuppence. You lot all drop small coins about like water. You don't know what they're for. It takes someone who knows the value of money to keep tuppence."

"Hetty, that's really quite good!" said Daisy.

"It's what they always say in my detective novels," said Mrs. Doherty. "Any detail, no matter how small, may be important."

"*Constant vigilance!*" chorused Hetty and Daisy, beaming at each other.

When Mrs. Doherty mentioned small details, I remembered the teacup, the watch, and the poisoned paper. These were the details that our whole case so far was based on, and this was our chance to find out more about at least one of them.

"The cup!" I said to Daisy. Luckily she understood me at once.

"What cup?" asked Mrs. Doherty.

I took another bite of tart so that I would not have to answer.

"Hazel's worried about the things from tea yesterday. She hates rats," Daisy said quickly. "Is it really *all* still in the dining room? You haven't tidied it up?"

At that moment Chapman came into the kitchens with a tray of glasses that clinked against each other. He peered around at us as though he wanted to tell us off. "What are you doing here, Miss Daisy?" he asked.

"Nothing!" said Daisy quickly. "Only talking to Mrs. Doherty and Hetty about . . . tea."

The glasses on Chapman's tray jangled together like out-of-tune bells, and he backed away against a row of cupboards as though Daisy had just brandished a knife at him.

"That's quite enough of *that*," he said, as if Daisy had said *murder* instead of *tea*. "Miss Daisy, take your friends out of these kitchens at once. Hetty and Mrs. Doherty have lunch to prepare, and I am a very busy man. *Now*, Miss Daisy!"

Once again we had to leave—but we had plenty to think about. It seemed to me that we had been given one extra clue. Although we knew that Chapman could not actually have been responsible for Mr. Curtis's murder, the way he had behaved when *tea* was mentioned made me think that he was worried about it. But why?

O ut we went into the hall—and stumbled onto
another scene. Lady Hastings, in the same bright
green dress and extravagant fur she had been
wearing the day before, was standing in the middle of the
worn hall carpet, and she was shouting at Uncle Felix.

"I'm in mourning!" she wailed. "Why can't anyone
understand that? Oh, I have a heartless family. You should
have heard Bertie just now, telling me I should be pleased
that Denis is dead. *Pleased!*"

"Don't exaggerate, Margaret," said Uncle Felix. "You
hardly knew him."

"*Hardly knew him!*" cried Lady Hastings. "I'll have you
know that he was my *everything!*"

Next to me, Daisy gasped. Her face had gone very pale.
"NO, HE WASN'T!" she shouted at her mother, her usual
composure cracking. "*DADDY IS!* Why do you have to
ruin everything?"

"Daisy!" gasped Lady Hastings, turning to face us. "What are you doing here? Didn't I tell you to go and play? Miss Alston! Miss Alston!"

"Really, Daisy, do get yourself under control," said Uncle Felix. "We can't have everyone losing their heads."

Daisy glared at him. "I *am* under control," she said. "Are you?"

"This family!" Lady Hastings threw up her hands theatrically and rushed away up the stairs.

At that moment Miss Alston stepped out of the music room. Of course, she must have heard her name being called, but seeing her still gave me a frightful shock. Daisy froze, Kitty gasped and Beanie gave a small, frightened squeal.

"What a lot of noise," said Miss Alston. "Whatever is it?"

I stared at her shiny brown handbag and wondered how on earth we would ever get it away from her.

"My sister, making a scene," said Uncle Felix, and he gave Miss Alston a curious look. I struggled to work out what it was . . . and then I had it. It was the sort of look Daisy gave me, to tell me what she was thinking without using words. It was a look between friends—but as far as I knew, Uncle Felix and Miss Alston had never met before this weekend.

"Miss Alston," he said, with another one of those curious looks, "I think the girls are bored."

"We are not!" said Daisy. "We're perfectly all right. Kitty and Beanie were going to help Mrs. D. set out the lunch things, and Hazel and I were about to take a quick walk in the garden. Weren't we, Hazel?"

"Oh," I said. "Yes."

"But—" Kitty began indignantly.

"It's spiffing of you to *assist* Mrs. D. like that," said Daisy. "Think of all the *useful things* you'll learn. Now, come along, Hazel."

She clamped her fingers around my wrist and dragged me toward the front door. Although she looked as cool as anything, I could feel her trembling. I turned and looked back at Miss Alston and Uncle Felix, and saw them still standing together, staring at us. This was suspicious behavior indeed. They were all I could think about at that moment, but I knew that Daisy had no room in her head for anything but her mother.

We hurried out through the heavy stone front doorway. It had stopped raining for a moment, but I shivered. What I wanted was some lunch—I was terribly jealous of Kitty and Beanie, able to help with it—but this was just between Daisy and me, like old times, and I knew I ought to appreciate it.

Daisy wrinkled her nose and strode out onto the lawn without a pause. The ground was sopping, and my shoes

Robin Stevens

sank into the grass. I tried to go on tiptoe to save them, but it was no good. I soon gave up and slopped after her.

"I hate Mummy," said Daisy, after a while. "I know I oughtn't to, but I *hate* her. Being sad about Mr. Curtis! Saying that he was more important to her than Daddy! She's horrid. *Oh!* What a disappointment she is. Perhaps the murderer *did* do us a favor, getting rid of Mr. Curtis. Now perhaps she'll forget about him, and everything can go back to the way it was."

"But he is *dead*, Daisy," I said, stumbling on a particularly slippery hummock of grass.

We passed the maze and went on outward toward the flooded fields, Fallingford House on its little hill receding behind us. I wished it were so easy to leave it behind for good.

"So?" asked Daisy. "Perhaps some people oughtn't to live."

My fists clenched, and I stopped. "*Daisy!*" I said. "Don't talk like that! You know it isn't true. Mr. Curtis was horrid, and what he and your mother were doing was awful, but he didn't deserve to *die* because of it! You mustn't say so."

"Well, someone thought he did," she replied. "What a horrible case this is! Everything's the wrong way round. The only really nasty person is dead. Just our luck, isn't it?"

At that moment a postage-stamp window flashed open in the house behind us, and a little doll person stuck its head out and yelled. For one unpleasant moment I thought something else terrible must have happened, but then I heard the words the little person—Kitty—was shouting.

"*Lunch!*" she cried, very small and far away. "*Come on in!*" and she wiggled her matchstick arms like semaphore. My stomach gave a glad rumble.

"Bother," said Daisy. "Meals. Why do they keep coming round to interrupt us? All right—after lunch we'll have a proper Detective Society meeting to discuss what we have discovered this morning. We'll have it in the Secret Tree, so that Bertie and Stephen can't come bothering us again. Are you in, Watson?"

"Are Kitty and Beanie in?" I asked. The Secret Tree sounded like outside, and outside, I could feel perfectly well, was still wet.

"Yes, they're in too," said Daisy, sighing. "If you insist. Although they aren't really necessary. That is to say, they aren't *you*."

"Oh," I said, suddenly feeling quite warm despite the chilly wind blowing through my cardigan.

"Don't speak," said Daisy. "Just shake on it."

So we did the Detective Society handshake, and then we ran (squelchily) in to lunch.

L unch was lamb, vegetables, creamy mashed potatoes, and a wobbly pink blancmange with cherries on top for dessert. While we were eating the lamb, Bertie made a joke about murderers, and Chapman dropped his serving platter and had to be helped by Hetty. Uncle Felix and Miss Alston shared yet more suspicious glances, and I thought again how very odd this weekend was turning out to be.

"All right," said Daisy, half an hour later.

The four of us were squashed into the crook of the big oak that stands just outside the walled garden, looking over onto fruit trees that had all of their early blooms shaken off by the storm. A few rotting boards had been knocked together to make a platform and a sort of roof, but they were green-smelling and slimy, and my seat was not at all comfortable. Every time I moved I got more black stains across my knees and arms. The sky was gray, and suspiciously damp-looking, but the rain was holding off for the moment.

"Order! Order! This meeting of the Detective Society is hereby convened. Beanie, stop wriggling."

"Sorry, Daisy," said Beanie. "I'll stop."

"This place is fearfully uncomfortable, Daisy," said Kitty. "Really, do we *have* to be here?"

"*Yes we do*. From up here we can see anyone coming—do you want the murderer to creep up on us unawares?"

"I don't like all this murder," said Beanie unhappily. "I wish there hadn't been one."

"Well, whether you like it or not, there has been," said Daisy, "and now it's up to us to work out who it was."

"I know," said Beanie. "I just don't like it."

Daisy rolled her eyes at Kitty, who smirked back. I thought this was rather cruel. After all, there was a bit of me that understood what Beanie meant. I love detecting, but I also love being safe. Daisy has a short memory for bad things. All she can remember from the Deepdean murder is the glory—none of the horrible nighttime chasing. Sometimes I can't get the chasing out of my head.

"All right," she said now. "We must now consider the new information we have gathered since our last meeting. What evidence do we have? The missing cup and watch. The scrap of paper from the book. And the forged documents.

"The missing cup and watch: Now, we've been over the

cup before, but I do wonder more and more why the *watch* was taken as well."

"Because it was pretty and valuable?" asked Beanie.

"It's possible," said Daisy. "And if it was that, the most likely suspect would be Aunt Saskia. We must check her room to see if the watch is hidden there.

"But there's someone else who's got a better motive to take the watch: Stephen."

I squashed my lips together, but all the same I couldn't prevent a small noise coming out.

Daisy rolled her eyes. "Hazel doesn't think he did it, of course, but even Hazel can be wrong. Now, Hetty and Mrs. D. confirmed what we already knew—that Stephen is poor. The watch is quite obviously dreadfully valuable—what if he stole it to pay debts, or something like that?"

"But how would we check?" I asked.

"Quite easily," said Daisy. "We use you. Go up to Stephen the very next chance you get and find out if he . . . needs money. He likes you, after all. He'll be honest."

I wouldn't do it! I thought. I would not, not even for Daisy. But then I remembered who the other suspects were. If Daisy was willing to suspect her family, then I must be brave enough to rule out her brother's friend.

I picked at the mold on the board next to me. Under my fingernails it turned quite black and foul. "Oh, all right," I said at last. "I'll ask him."

"Excellent," said Daisy. "Look, the watch may be a blind. The murderer may just have taken it on a whim, or by mistake. We must consider the other evidence too.

"Like that bit of paper you found on the dining room table. It was torn out of a book of poetry, and judging by that smudge on it, it's likely that the murderer used it to keep the poison in until they poured it into Mr. Curtis's tea. Unfortunately, this is less helpful than it seems. Mummy and Daddy aren't very bookish, but they could still have gone into the library and torn out a page—and any of the others might have had a book on them at the crucial moment."

"But isn't it more likely to be someone who *does* read?" I asked. "Like . . . Uncle Felix."

Daisy frowned. "I suppose so. Yes. And even I have to admit that Uncle Felix has been behaving in a . . . thoroughly un-uncle-like manner. He's still lying about what he thinks happened to Mr. Curtis, and doing everything he can to stop Mummy calling the police."

"And—Daisy," I said, "I think he might know Miss Alston. The way they looked at each other just now . . . I really don't think they've only just met."

"If all you have to base that on is looks—" Daisy began, but then Kitty cut in.

"Oh yes, I thought so too!" she said. "They looked awfully friendly when we saw them before lunch, didn't they?"

Daisy narrowed her eyes at both of us. She was outnumbered, and she wasn't used to it. "Hmm," she said. "Perhaps. We must watch Uncle Felix, I admit that—although I don't think it can be him. Even if he's been behaving oddly, we know he's *good*, just the way we knew Mr. Curtis was *bad*."

I frowned. I wasn't sure that we *did* know that.

"I do think that it's less likely to be Mummy. If I was a bad detective who only went on feelings—not that this applies to anyone *here*"—she glared at us—"I'd rule her out because she's simply too upset about Mr. Curtis dying, and because she contacted the police when no one else wanted to. But of course, we must be entirely rigorous. We need evidence of her innocence, and we don't have that yet. Perhaps if we conducted a re-creation of the crime scene, we might be able to rule her, or another suspect, out . . . Yes, let's put that down on our to-do list.

"Now, the forged documents. These are terribly important bits of evidence, as they confirm that Miss Alston is not who she seems to be. She is at Fallingford under some sort of assumed identity. But why? Hazel and I witnessed Mr. Curtis threatening her outside the maze on Saturday morning. He seemed to know who she was—did she kill him to prevent him telling Mummy and Daddy her secret?

"We must discover her true identity—and after what Mrs. D. said, our best chance must be to get hold of that handbag of hers and see what she's got hidden in there. I want to find out what was on that paper that Hazel and I saw her hiding—it may be very important."

She stared around at us, eyes wide, and we all nodded.

"Now, before we end, is there any new bit of evidence we've missed?"

"Um," I said, "should we be watching Chapman? He's behaving awfully oddly. What if he knows something?"

"Oh!" said Beanie. "You mean—how nervous he seemed today?"

"Yes!" I said. "And lots of other things."

"That's an excellent thought, Hazel!" said Daisy. "Why, he might be protecting someone. Like . . ."

But then she paused. We both realized, then, who Chapman would be most likely to shield. Someone from Daisy's family—and not just that, but someone who was part of Fallingford itself. That meant Lady Hastings, Bertie—or Lord Hastings. Lord Hastings, I thought, who we had all seen shouting at Mr. Curtis on the morning of the murder.

"Who?" asked Beanie, wide-eyed. "Who do you mean?"

Daisy and I looked at each other—and thankfully, at that moment, it began to rain. At first it was only a soft stumble on the leaves high above us, but then it gathered to a sigh, a swish, and finally a roar.

"Inside!" cried Daisy as Kitty held up her hands to cover her hair. She is fearfully vain sometimes, and Daisy knows that. We were saved.

Robin Stevens

We scrambled down the tree trunk, slipping and sliding and getting our hands all smeared with horrid black mold. "This meeting is adjourned!" shrieked Daisy. "Now to move on to the next part of our investigation—ruling out suspects! Oh, I do like this bit!"

We pelted across the lawn. My hair draggled about my face and the rain blurred everything in front of me like mist. As we dashed through the lashes of rain toward the front door, I wondered again whether we really *wanted* to know what had happened to Mr. Curtis. After all, he was a very nasty person. Whoever had killed him was far nicer than he could ever be—and they might be someone very important to Daisy. I felt guilty for thinking it—but how could Mr. Curtis's murderer deserve to be hanged?

Part Four
Things Begin to Look Rather Black

We came stumbling into the hall, shrieking and spilling water onto the stone floor, Daisy shaking her golden head like a dog—just in time to see something extremely curious. Miss Alston was standing at the foot of the main stairs speaking to Stephen. She was leaning forward in quite an intense manner, eyes fixed on him, and although she kept her voice down I managed to catch the phrase *if you saw anything . . .*

Stephen looked terrified. His face was white, and his freckles stood out, livid. I was alarmed. What had we overheard? I glanced at Daisy, eyes wide, to see what she made of it. This certainly was even more suspicious behavior from Miss Alston. It sounded to me as though she was threatening Stephen. Why? Did she think he had seen something crucial to the mystery? Was she trying to make him reveal what he knew? Or . . . did she want to make sure he kept silent?

Miss Alston spun round and stared at us. Her brown handbag was, as always, clutched to her chest, and I wondered how on earth Daisy thought we would ever be able to get it away from her. "What's all this noise?" she asked. "Girls, what were you doing outside in the rain? You'll catch your deaths!"

Beanie shrieked. Kitty slapped her. I could not help gasping a little. After all the things we had been thinking about Miss Alston, this turn of phrase sounded most sinister. If she was the murderer, *catching our deaths* was exactly what she wanted us to do. The idea of sitting with her for a lesson made me feel utterly terrified.

Miss Alston narrowed her eyes at us, and I tried to breathe normally. "Hmm," she said at last. "I shall call Mrs. Doherty to come and help you get dried off. And then lessons, girls! Daisy, your mother doesn't want you sitting about moping."

"We're not moping!" she said quickly. "We're busy. Can't we have just a few more hours? I don't think I could bear a lesson now."

Miss Alston puffed out a breath. "Oh, very well," she said. "Two hours. But I want you in the music room at five o'clock precisely. Otherwise I shall come and *find* you."

We all took a step backward. Miss Alston frowned. "*Mrs. Doherty!*" she called, and Mrs. Doherty came running out of the kitchens.

Robin Stevens

She gasped when she saw us. "Good Lord!" she cried. "Hetty! Towels, quick!"

We were wrapped up in piles of faded and slightly horsy-smelling towels.

"Whatever were you doing?" asked Mrs. Doherty, scrubbing away at Daisy's hair.

Miss Alston waited to see that we were being attended to, and then she went up the stairs, handbag swinging from her arm as always. I was glad that she was gone—but where was she going? What was she going to do with the time until five o'clock?

Stephen was turning away too. "Stephen!" I called, as quietly as I could. "Are you . . . ? Are you all right?" I wanted to ask, *Was Miss Alston threatening you?*—but of course I couldn't, and so what came out sounded weak and strange.

"Oh yes," said Stephen, coming toward me so that we could talk without the others hearing. "Rather looking forward to going back to school, though, after all this."

I nodded fervently. I couldn't even say how much I agreed with him.

"Funny," he went on, smiling. "I never thought I'd say that. Scholarship boy, you know. It can be rather hard when you're sharing a dorm with two lords and a viscount. If Bertie hadn't taken up with me I'd have run away years ago."

"I didn't know you were on a scholarship," I said. My

heart was hammering. What I was discovering was quite the opposite of what I had expected. "Will you . . . ? What about university? Will you go?"

"Scholarship again," said Stephen. "I only heard last month. I'm disgustingly lucky, really." He made a funny face, half ashamed, half happy. "We aren't rich, not like *here*, but we get by. *You* know."

I blushed. I didn't know. As well as the wedding-cake compound, my father has a yacht and his own office building in the middle of Hong Kong, and we have ten times more servants than Daisy's family. But it is easy to hide that under the skin of not being English.

"Er, yes," I said, hating myself a bit. "Of course. I'm glad you're all right."

Stephen smiled at me, and then went hurrying up the stairs to find Bertie. I could hardly believe my luck. Stephen had a scholarship now, and another for university next year. He didn't need money. There was no reason for him to steal the watch—and therefore no reason for him to kill Mr. Curtis. I was flooded with relief.

Robin Stevens

II

As soon as Mrs. Doherty and Hetty had gone, Daisy spun around. "Quick!" she hissed. "Now, while we still can! It's the perfect opportunity!"

"For what?" asked Kitty.

"*To do some more investigating,*" whispered Daisy. "After all, we agreed we needed to look in Aunt Saskia's room, didn't we?"

We slipped up the stairs, holding our breath and trying not to bump into each other. I took hold of Daisy's sleeve as we climbed.

"Daisy!" I whispered. "Did you hear what Stephen just said to me? He's on a scholarship, and he'll have another one at university. He doesn't need money! I think we can rule him out."

Daisy looked at me, and the wrinkle appeared at the top of her nose.

"You ought to be pleased," I said, a bit crossly—though as

soon as I had said it, I saw that it was me who was pleased, and me only. If it wasn't Stephen, then there was more chance that it was someone in Daisy's family. I flushed, and let go of her arm again.

Aunt Saskia's little room was just at the top of the stairs, but as I turned toward it I stared across the landing at Mr. Curtis's locked door, and couldn't help shuddering. To think that there was a dead body in there!

Aunt Saskia's door was unlocked. When Daisy pushed it, it gaped open, and the room beyond was dark, curtains still pulled across the windows, although I could hear the rain rattling against them outside.

"Golly!" breathed Kitty. "Look at these *things*!"

Silk scarves and crushed-velvet skirts lay scattered across the floor or draped across chairs, drooping down to brush the green carpet. Mangy furs lay everywhere, looking unpleasantly dead, and on the dressing table groups of bottles and jars and pots were covered with dirty handkerchiefs and powder puffs.

I had thought the rest of Fallingford rather untidy, but this was beyond anything. I could hardly believe that Aunt Saskia had only been here two days.

"All right, Detectives," said Daisy. "Let's hunt. Our targets, as discussed, are Mr. Curtis's watch and his teacup. And, if possible, a book with a torn-out page."

I looked around—and didn't quite know where to begin.

Robin Stevens

I couldn't imagine anywhere less like Miss Alston's tidy room. There could have been an army of watches and cups hidden under these clothes. But Daisy dived into a pile of blouses with gusto, and soon Kitty was following her lead. While Beanie sifted uneasily through the contents of the dressing table, poking at a pile of lipstick-smeared tissues, I began to peek under the pillows. The bed smelled of stale old lady, and I wrinkled my nose unhappily.

"Oh, hurry up, Hazel," said Daisy, and she came up beside me, shoved aside the bolster and then wormed her fingers under Aunt Saskia's mattress.

"Nothing here," she grunted, wriggling farther and farther in, until her shoulder was almost swallowed up by the heavy mattress. "Nothing . . . nothing . . . Ooh, what's *this?*"

The rest of us stopped searching and looked over at her.

"Is it the watch?" Kitty asked.

"No!" said Daisy. "At least—it doesn't seem like the right shape . . . Wait a moment!"

She backed out from under the mattress, and spilling out of her hands was a glitter of jewels, a shine of gold, a jangling pile of necklaces and earrings and bracelets.

"Mummy's necklace!" said Daisy. "Daddy's cuff links! And—oh, look, she's even pinched the silver decanter tags! Goodness, I thought she only stole spoons!"

"I can't see Mr. Curtis's watch," I said.

"That's because it isn't here," said Daisy, shifting her

hands. "*Bother!* Mind you, I think everything else is. Some of these things aren't even ours! Lord, I never knew she'd got this bad."

"What does it mean?" asked Kitty.

"It means that we now know the reason why Aunt Saskia doesn't want Mummy to call the police. She's a kleptomaniac!"

"Someone who can't resist stealing things," I whispered to Beanie, who was wrinkling up her brow.

"Imagine if the police found all this! Not even Daddy could save Aunt Saskia from being arrested. She's obviously quite unhinged—why, some of these things are worth simply pots and pots of money. They must be fearfully important to her—I couldn't before, but now I really can imagine her killing a person for a beautiful thing she wanted. And we all saw that she wanted the watch."

Kitty and Beanie looked fearfully at each other, and I saw Kitty shiver. What horrible things people did, I thought. Being a detective meant that you had to face some truly dreadful crimes.

"But if the cup and watch aren't here, doesn't that rule her out?" asked Beanie.

"No, worse luck!" said Daisy, shifting from foot to foot restlessly. "She might simply have hidden them somewhere else. Botheration! Most of our suspects seem more guilty, not less, the more we discover about them. What to do?"

Robin Stevens

It was not the sort of question you answered—but Kitty didn't know that.

"I think we should do that re-creation of the crime you were talking about," she said. "It sounds better than ferreting about in people's rooms, even if we do find jewels."

"Oh yes, can we stop doing illegal things for a while?" asked Beanie. "It gives me the funnies. I'm *sure* we'll be caught!"

"Assistant members of the Detective Society"—Daisy saw me making a face—"can sometimes come up with ideas that aren't *entirely* terrible," she finished. "In fact, Kitty, that was exactly what I was about to suggest."

"But how are we going to do it?" I remembered our re-creation in the Deepdean gym last year. "The dining room's locked!"

"Well, the *real* dining room is," said Daisy, "but I happen to have a secret weapon. For my eighth birthday Mummy had a Fallingford dollhouse made for me—an absolutely perfect replica, with all the furniture and the back stairs, and a tiny me and Mummy and Daddy and Bertie to live in it. It's still up in the nursery."

"Oh, I know!" said Beanie, beaming. "Kitty was playing with it when you were out of the room."

"I was *not!*" cried Kitty, going red. "I was only admiring it."

"Anyway, we can use the replica dining room to set up

our murder scene. There's a tiny Aunt Saskia and a tiny Uncle Felix too, and a Chapman, and we can use some of the other dolls to stand in for Stephen, Miss Alston, and Mr. Curtis."

It was a very good plan—and importantly, it would get us out of Aunt Saskia's room. Daisy stuffed the jewels back under the mattress, and we all went galloping up the front stairs—no need for quiet this time—to the nursery.

T he dollhouse was pushed to the very edge of the
room, its heavy wooden front hanging open in a
lonely way, its painted outside walls peeling. It was
like Fallingford in miniature, dusty but absolutely perfect. I
stared down at the stairs and doors and rooms all piled on
top of each other, and felt like a giant, or a god, or both.

As we watched, Daisy crouched down busily in front of
the house and shifted furniture about with a series of loud
clicks.

"There!" she said at last, sitting back on her heels, and
we peered over her shoulder at the tiny dining room. I saw
everything the way it had been on Saturday afternoon: tiny
chairs, tiny lamps and even a tiny toy tea laid out on the
little table. I saw a plate of cakes smaller than my fingernail,
and teacups I barely wanted to breathe on in case I blew
them away. It gave me quite a creepy feeling, as though
I were seeing backward in time. I hoped that none of the

grown-ups (and here I was really thinking of Miss Alston) came in to see what we were doing.

"Now!" cried Daisy, breaking into my thoughts. "We all agree that the murderer took poison from the hall cupboard, put some in a bit of paper and brought it into the dining room like that, yes?"

I shivered. I could just imagine it—the murderer pausing in front of the hall cupboard, and a horrible idea creeping into their head. They would have been quite safe from suspicion too—I've seen in that cupboard, and it's so full of useful things, like string and bootblack and clothes brushes, that they could simply have pretended to be looking for something else if they were caught there.

"So," said Daisy. "Now let's see just how easy it is to get poison from a bit of paper into a cup of tea. For this bit we shan't need the dollhouse. We'll re-create it ourselves. My bedside table can be the tea table, and we'll use that tooth mug as the cup. You three go and stand round it, and I'll sit on Hazel's bed, and be Mr. Curtis in his chair. Hazel, rip out a bit of your casebook to be the paper filled with poison, and we're ready."

I was glad that I didn't have to play the part of the murder victim this time, the way I did for our last case. It felt too dangerous, as though I were asking to be murdered myself.

"I want you to choose someone to be the murderer. Quietly, so I can't hear you. Then I want the murderer to

Robin Stevens

pick a moment to open the paper over the cup and pretend to tip poison in. As soon as you've done that, shout—and let's see if you can manage it without me noticing. Are you ready?"

The three of us got into a huddle beside the table.

"Who does it?" hissed Kitty. "Me? I'm sure I could do it—do let me, it's most awful fun—"

"No," I whispered back. Beanie was wriggling desperately, eyes wide, and I could tell that she was itching to do something important. "Let Beanie."

"Me?" gasped Beanie. "Oh, *goody!*"

"*Do* keep it down," said Daisy from my bed—or rather, Mr. Curtis's chair. "I'm trying to hum, but you're nearly drowning me out."

"Yes, you!" I whispered. "You can do it! I know you can! And think, you'd be able to say that you'd tricked Daisy!"

"Oh, I don't think I like the sound of that," said Beanie unhappily. "It's not very nice. Are you sure . . . ? Oh—oh, all right. Don't pinch me, Kitty. I'll try."

"We're ready," I called over to Daisy. Then Kitty and I began to jostle and elbow each other and Beanie; we reached across the little table, using both hands to scoop up imaginary cream buns and slices of cake. It was surprisingly good fun, and even Beanie, who squeaked at first, got quite carried away. The tooth mug was just by Kitty's hip, and I was so busy fighting with her over a particularly delicious muffin, dripping with butter (I wouldn't have minded a real muffin or two, if it came to it), that I hardly noticed the moment when Beanie held the little piece of paper in her fist over the mug.

Daisy kept on humming, and when we turned to her a minute later she looked cross. "Haven't you done it yet?" she asked.

"I *have!*" cried Beanie. "Ooh, didn't you see me? How exciting! It was quite easy . . . Oh dear, I've just pretended to *murder* someone."

"Don't worry, Beans," said Kitty, patting her comfortingly on the shoulder. "You did excellently well. It wasn't real, you know."

"Did you really do it?" asked Daisy. "Heavens! Then it *must* have been easy. Do you know, I didn't see a thing. There was such a scrum."

"And I hardly noticed either," I put in, "even though I knew it was going to happen. So we've proved that it isn't odd at all that none of the other people noticed the poison going in the cup."

"This is all going extremely well," said Daisy, satisfied. She stood up and went over to the dollhouse. "Now, the next step is to really think back to that crucial moment, and for this we *do* need the house. Let's put all the suspects in the places they were on Saturday afternoon. This ugly doll is Mr. Curtis, and this little one can be Stephen.

We don't need dolls for the three of you, because it's quite obvious that you were standing next to me, away from the table—remember, we hadn't begun to eat then. We were holding back."

We all crouched round the dollhouse together. It was very strange—like a silly childish game but at the same time deadly serious. The Mr. Curtis doll (who really was hideous) went in the chair, away from the tea table. Daisy put Chapman back against the wall, on the other side of the room from Mr. Curtis. Then we positioned Lord and Lady Hastings, Uncle Felix, Bertie, Stephen, and Aunt Saskia around the tea table, just where they had all been.

"Chatter chatter chatter," said Daisy, bouncing the Bertie doll up and down in her hand. "Scuffle, scuffle—Aunt Saskia goes for the tarts . . ." She made Aunt Saskia doll lunge for them, and I nearly laughed. "Mummy says, 'I'll be Mother,' but everyone ignores her"—Kitty made the Lady Hastings doll wobble—"then she says, 'Someone fetch Mr. Curtis a cup of tea,' and then—"

I suddenly had a rush of memory—of Lord Hastings's round red face, and the expression on it, and of his hand *holding out a teacup.*

I was holding the Lord Hastings doll, his little face as jolly as it usually is in real life. But it hadn't been jolly then. His expression had been . . . sly, odd, as though he had done something wrong and he knew it. I didn't want it to be true, but I knew I had to be honest about what I'd seen.

"Then Lord Hastings hands a cup of tea to Mr. Curtis, and he drinks it," I said.

The Bertie doll froze. Daisy had gone quite still. Outside, the rain seemed to grow even louder.

"Ugh!" said Beanie in a little doll voice, prodding Mr. Curtis. "This tea tastes foul!"

We all looked at her, and I felt quite heartsick. "He did say that!" she told us defensively. "I was only remembering."

"I know he did," said Daisy, jumping back into life. "I—excellent memory. And Hazel. Yes. You too. What a . . . What I mean to say is—"

It was one of the few times I had ever seen Daisy stumbling.

"But perhaps the poison was already in the cup by then," she said at last, blinking. "Someone else at the table must have put it in and then handed the cup to Daddy to give to Mr. Curtis."

"Lord Hastings did look funny, though," said Beanie. "All shifty, like he'd been naughty."

I knew she was telling the truth—I remembered it too—but all the same I suddenly wanted to shake her. How could she not see what this meant for Daisy?

A heavy feeling had settled on my chest. I really and truly liked Lord Hastings, even if he did tell dreadful jokes.

Robin Stevens

He was nice to me, and he was Daisy's father. I didn't want him to have killed horrible Mr. Curtis. But there it was. We had discovered that he had handed Mr. Curtis the cup of tea that had killed him.

"Well," said Daisy, and her voice was very tight. I saw her hands clench in her lap. "Well . . . it . . . I tell you, it simply *must* have been someone else who gave it to him to pass on. Daddy knows perfectly well not to murder his own guests, however rude they are. Look—what about Chapman? Hazel, you said yourself that he'd been behaving oddly. Just look where he's standing. He would have been able to see the table, and people's hands. He must have seen something—which means that we must go and speak to him. He'll be able to rule Daddy out. If Daddy *was* looking shifty, I'm quite sure it was for another reason altogether."

I could hear the relief in her voice as she said it, but I was not so sure. I was terribly afraid that, if Daisy spoke to Chapman, she was not likely to enjoy what she heard.

IV

At first, Chapman proved difficult to find. "He ought to be around here somewhere," said Daisy crossly, popping in and out of doorways on the second floor like a jack-in-the-box. "Oh! Hello, Chapman!"

Chapman was in Lord Hastings's bedroom, standing on wobbly tiptoes at the window and dusting. He jumped at Daisy's voice, and the duster fell out of his hand and clattered on the floor.

"Hello, Chapman," said Daisy. "How are you?"

"Very well, Miss Daisy," he replied automatically.

"We want to ask you a question," said Daisy. "It's about Mr. Curtis."

Chapman swayed, his face creasing up as though he had been hurt—he looked just as frightened as he had in the kitchens earlier. "Who else have you been talking to?" he cried. "What have they said?"

"Why, no one!" said Daisy. "It's only that Daddy's been

in such a funny mood since . . . you know—and I'm terribly worried that he's got a silly idea in his head that he had something to do with what happened. Of course, I know he didn't! You must have seen it—can't you reassure him?"

Chapman went bone-white. He was shaking too; he looked as if he were about to break apart.

"I didn't . . . see . . . anything," he whispered. "Not a thing! I didn't look and I couldn't have seen."

Daisy looked puzzled. "But, Chapman, don't be so silly! You must have!"

"I didn't . . . see . . . anything," Chapman repeated, "and if I did—well, that man was purely wicked. Sometimes the truth doesn't make things better. Now, out of this room at once."

Daisy flushed with annoyance. "It's not fair of you, Chapman!" she cried.

"I'm not saying anything more," said Chapman resolutely. "Go on, go away. I've got work to do."

Daisy went pink, then white, then pink again, and she turned and rushed out of the room.

We hurried after her, but we were barely halfway across the second-floor landing when Lord Hastings himself came panting up the main stairs, exactly as though he had been summoned. He gave us all a distracted wave, then darted off into his bedroom.

"Ah, Chapman!" we heard him say. "Just the man I wanted to see."

Daisy paused. Then she turned to me. "Quick!" she hissed. "We have to listen in!"

"Ought we to?" asked Beanie in concern.

"Of course not," said Daisy. "But I've told you before, that's the point of detection."

She crept closer, right up to the door—which, in his hurry, Lord Hastings had not managed to close properly. I wanted to back away again, but Daisy's hand was round my wrist, and I knew I had to stay, to hear what she was about to hear.

". . . wanted to, er, clear up any misconceptions that might have . . . that is . . . Chapman, old thing, what I'm trying to say is that, if you *did* see anything at the tea that might have given you cause for concern, anything that I—"

"It never happened, sir," said Chapman. "There was nothing to see."

"Yes!" said Lord Hastings, his voice warm with relief. "That's it exactly. Nothing happened. Nothing to see. And that's what you'll say, should anyone ask?"

"That is what I will say, sir."

"Good man. Excellent man! That's . . . It's above and beyond, Chapman, simply above and beyond everything. This shan't be forgotten."

"Sir, if I may, I shall forget it immediately," said Chapman. "May I go, sir?"

Robin Stevens

We all jumped back automatically—all except Daisy. She simply stood there, eyes blank.

"*Hide!*" I hissed, because someone had to do *something*, and Daisy seemed to have frozen up completely.

We all dived in different directions, and I ended up in the alcove behind the stuffed owl, right arm linked with Daisy's and dizzily breathing in dust from the curtain.

Lord Hastings's heavy feet went thundering across the landing, and then down the stairs—followed, a few moments later, by Chapman's soft, precise steps. We were alone.

I thought again about what we had just heard: Lord Hastings asking for Chapman's help, making sure that he didn't tell anyone what he had seen. It fitted—horribly— with our re-creation. Had Chapman seen Lord Hastings slipping something into the cup before he handed it to Mr. Curtis? I did not want it to be true, but what else was I to think?

"Daisy," I said thickly because of my heart and the curtains, "your father—"

"Oh, I know," Daisy whispered, coming back to herself with a twitch. Her voice was falsely bright. I could tell that she had decided to keep on pretending. "The old silly's done something, and he doesn't want to be found out. Isn't Chapman a brick?"

"But—"

"Oh goodness," said Daisy. "It won't be about the *murder*, Hazel! Don't be a chump. I've said before, Daddy wouldn't do it!"

I realized that Daisy's incredible calm about the case was really just another front. She could pretend to suspect her brother, and her mother, and her uncle—and I don't think she even minded about suspecting her great-aunt. But she was only playing when it came to Bertie and Lady Hastings and Uncle Felix; she wouldn't even play about her father. There were some thoughts that she refused to let in—and although I was achingly sorry for her as a friend, as a detective I knew that she simply had to face up to them. Daisy, I thought to myself, was not going to ruin *this* case because she didn't like the way it was going.

As I decided that, something pinged loose inside me, like a button popping off a tight skirt. I took hold of Daisy's shoulders and pulled her round to face me.

"Yes he would!" I cried. "He would just as much as anyone! We know he didn't like Mr. Curtis, and he knew about Mr. Curtis and your mother—we saw him arguing with Mr. Curtis yesterday morning. And I *saw* him, Daisy. I saw him hand the cup of tea to Mr. Curtis! He's the most likely of anyone to be the murderer! I didn't want to believe it—but now, after what we heard, we have to!"

Robin Stevens

Daisy opened her mouth. There was an angry flush across her cheeks. "How dare you, Hazel!" she said.

"I'm your vice president!" I said. "I have to say it—no one else will! And if you don't listen to me, you're not being a proper Detective Society president!"

As soon as the words were out of my mouth, I knew that I had said something very wrong.

"Get out of my way," hissed Daisy. "Take your hands off of me."

"But don't you know—"

"OF COURSE I KNOW, YOU IDIOT!" she shrieked. "WHY COULDN'T YOU HAVE LET ME PRETEND?"

She threw herself at me. I staggered, the curtain ripped, and I fell backward, heavily, onto the landing, Daisy half on top of me.

"I'm going to the nursery," she said. "Don't bother to follow me." Then she scrambled to her feet and dashed away up the stairs, golden braids bouncing behind her.

Beanie and Kitty had crawled out of their hiding places, and they were staring at me with almost identical expressions of horror.

"What happened?" whispered Beanie. "Is Daisy all right?"

"I told her that Lord Hastings might be the murderer," I said.

"Cruel," said Kitty, "but true."

"Don't," I said. I was in no mood for Kitty's nasty side.

"Ooh, all right, Hazel Wong," said Kitty, holding up her hands. "What do you propose your precious Detective Society does, now that Daisy's gone off in a sulk?"

I took a slightly wobbly breath. What *were* we to do?

"We . . . ," I said. "We're going to—"

And then we heard the most terrible crash.

Robin Stevens

The three of us went running down the stairs (me wondering if it was particularly wise to run *toward* a noise when there was a murderer on the loose). There were no more smashes after the first one, but I realized that it had come from the kitchens. Beanie hung back, shaking her head in fear, and I knew that with no Daisy, I would have to give the orders.

"Come on," I said to her encouragingly. "We have to see what it is."

We went into the kitchens. Hetty was standing there, arms up to her chest. Broken crockery lay scattered around her feet, and Mrs. Doherty was next to her, openmouthed. They were both staring fixedly at the pile of dirty china beside the washing-up bowl.

"I'm not going mad," said Hetty to Mrs. Doherty. "I'm not."

"You certainly are *not*," said Mrs. Doherty firmly.

"Oh, what is it?" whispered Beanie. "Is it something awful?"

Mrs. Doherty turned and saw us. "Girls!" she said. "Goodness, isn't Daisy with you?"

"She's not feeling well," I said hurriedly. "What's happened?"

"It's . . . ," said Hetty. "Well, all the teacups from the good set, they're still in the dining room, and the dining room is *locked*, and has been since yesterday. But . . . look at *that*." And she pointed to the pile of washing-up.

We all squinted. The cups resting on top of each other looked very much like cups to me—until I saw that one of them was thinner than the others and fluted, with a fine band of gold around its rim and more on its sides.

"It's one of the good set, in *here*," Hetty said. "I don't understand it! It's impossible, but there it is. I shouldn't have dropped my tray—it was the shock. You see, I'd been thinking about *what happened* all day and then, suddenly, there was a reminder in front of me, and I don't see how it could have got there!"

Of course, I saw. There was only one explanation: the murderer must have slipped into the kitchens when Mrs. Doherty and Hetty were out and put the cup in among the washing-up, where they hoped no one would notice it. Lord Hastings had been downstairs just now, I remembered—we had seen him coming up to his bedroom to speak to Chapman.

"What's all this, what's all this?" boomed a large voice behind us. It was Lord Hastings again.

Beanie flinched and stepped back into Kitty, and I clenched my fists at my sides. After what we had overheard, I couldn't help it. If he really *was* the murderer, all his jolly goodness suddenly seemed like a lie.

"Is everything all right? What have you broken this time?" he asked.

"It was another rat, sir," said Mrs. Doherty composedly. "Hetty was startled, and she dropped a tray."

"Good grief, is that all? I should have thought you'd be used to them by now. Buck up, Hetty."

"Yes, sir," said Hetty. "I'm sorry, sir. It's a phobia."

"Goodness," said Lord Hastings. "Phobias! Don't believe in them myself. New-age mumbo jumbo. But still . . . don't do it again, eh?"

"No, sir," said Hetty.

Lord Hastings withdrew. We all heard him say to someone in the hall, "Hetty saw a rat. Says she has a *phobia*."

We all breathed again. "*Phobia*," said Mrs. Doherty. "I agree with Lord Hastings! But it is *odd*, all the same. I don't blame you for being shocked. Where *is* Daisy? It's not like her to miss a bit of excitement."

"She's not feeling well," I said again uncomfortably. "I'll . . . go and see her now."

I left Beanie and Kitty in the kitchens—they would be safe with Mrs. Doherty, I decided—and went upstairs alone. Some talks are for best friends only.

I climbed the back stairs to the nursery—I'd got into the habit of using them now—with a sick feeling in my stomach and a very leaden feeling in my feet. I didn't want to see Daisy, and I knew that she didn't want to see me. What if she never wanted to speak to me again?

I wondered whether we *should* give up on hunting for the murderer. After all, no one apart from Lady Hastings was upset about Mr. Curtis, and even she would probably get over it in time. I felt terrible for thinking it, but there it was.

I decided to tell Daisy that we were going to pretend none of this had ever happened. We didn't even need to pay attention to the cup. The police could look at it when they arrived.

But when I pushed open the door of the nursery, it seemed to be empty. I stared about in astonishment. Where had Daisy gone?

Then I heard a little rustling noise from under her bed. I got down on hands and knees and crawled cautiously forward—and saw a white sock, kicking against the metal bed frame. It was attached to a small ankle, and that was attached to a slim, scratched leg—and above that was Daisy's woolen skirt.

"Hello," I whispered. Very carefully, I put out a hand to tap Daisy's knee, and she turned her head and looked at me.

Her gold was all dimmed, and there were snaky dust tracks down her cheeks. At that moment she did not look like *my* Daisy Wells at all. "Go away," she said.

"I won't," I said. "Don't try to make me."

"What happened downstairs just now?" asked Daisy. "No! For all I care, you can solve the rotten case on your own. Since you're such a good detective, you won't be needing me anyway."

"You're a good detective too," I said loyally.

"Honestly, Hazel, don't be so *nice*." She pushed herself up onto her elbows and screwed up her face in despair. "Why can't everything be neat and simple and right?"

"I don't know," I said.

"It always is in books," said Daisy. "That's what upsets me. Somehow you don't expect . . . real life."

"It might not be *him*."

"Hazel, I need to buck up and face the facts," she said bitterly. "Oh, I could kill Mr. Curtis all over again for upsetting us all like this! What *was* that crash, by the way?"

"The missing teacup—Hetty's found it. It's back in the kitchens. Someone put it with the washing-up, among lots of other cups."

Daisy's head bumped against the bedsprings. "What?" she said. "It's back?"

"Yes. I'm sorry, Daisy. It's all muddled in with the other dirty things, so we won't be able to use it as evidence now."

But Daisy didn't look sorry at all. Suddenly she was fizzing, all her Daisy-ishness back with a vengeance.

"But, *Hazel!*" she cried. "Don't you see? This changes everything! If the teacup is in the kitchens, then Daddy simply didn't do the murder."

I didn't follow. "Daisy, your father was downstairs just now. He could easily have put the cup back in the kitchens."

Daisy bounced, and the bedsprings clinked again. She edged out from under the bed. "Ouch. No, Hazel, *listen*. It wouldn't occur to Daddy to put the teacup back where it ought to go. If he'd taken it, he'd keep it hidden . . . oh, I don't know, in his wardrobe, or do something silly and dramatic like burying it in the garden. He'd never hide it somewhere as sensible as the kitchens. This is the evidence I was hoping for. He's *innocent!*"

I thought about Lord Hastings's untidiness: his jackets and walking sticks and hats were scattered all over the house. Daisy is not always logical, but she has a sense about people, and in this case I realized that her sense might be right.

"But who did it, if he didn't?" I asked.

"Well," said Daisy, "Miss Alston has a tremendously tidy mind. And . . . let's see . . . Aunt Saskia behaves as though she's too silly for words, but really she is perfectly intelligent and resourceful. Hazel, I was wrong. We can't stop now—we simply can't! Daddy looks guilty—I see that, and that's what the police will think, once they arrive. What happened to the teacup proves to *me* that he didn't do it, but it won't prove anything to anyone official. We have to save him from himself! Daddy gets so terribly nervous—once some silly old lord asked him a question in the middle of a speech in the House of Lords, and Daddy got apoplectic and called him an *insufferable popinjay* in front of everyone. He refused to answer anything and had to be disciplined."

"What is a popinjay?" I asked.

"Goodness—a sort of parrot, don't you know? The point is, we've seen from our re-creation, and from our investigation in general, how guilty Daddy looks. The police will fix on him at once, and then he'll respond by behaving like the guiltiest man alive. If we don't help him, he'll be in jail in the blink of an eye."

"All right," I said. I did not share Daisy's dislike of the police, but I knew I had to back her up—and I did see what she meant about Lord Hastings. "But what shall we do about it?"

"Well, for the moment you'll just have to trust me," said Daisy, brushing herself down in a most businesslike manner. "Come on, let's go down and find our assistants, so we can inform them about this important development. We've ruled out another suspect!"

But as I raced to follow Daisy down the stairs, I couldn't help worrying. I believed her about the teacup, but I didn't see how we could prove it. And even if it was not Lord Hastings, that left five suspects, four of them in Daisy's family. I still felt that this case was not one that we would like solving. All the same, I was glad that the Daisy in front of me was my Daisy again, ridiculous and brilliant and mad— and superstitiously, I felt that Daisy in *that* sort of mood could solve anything.

As we reached the bottom of the stairs, the hall telephone rang, and Chapman limped out of the drawing room to answer it. He stared at us with a not-particularly-friendly expression on his face.

"Hello?" he said. "Indeed it is . . . Yes . . . No . . . Yes—certainly, sir, I shall just fetch her." Then he held the mouthpiece away from his face as though it might bite him, and called, "Madam! Telephone!"

There was no answer, and Chapman sighed, put down the receiver, and shuffled away toward the library. As soon as he'd gone, Daisy pounced. She was obviously still in an extremely buoyant mood. She pressed the receiver to her ear and the mouthpiece to her lips and shouted, "Hello! Inspector Priestley? Hello . . . ? Oh, who is this . . . ? No, I'm not Lady Hastings. Goodness, how old do you think I am? Who are you? Where's Inspector Priestley? You're being awfully lax, you know—you should tell your inspector that if he doesn't hurry up and get here quickly we will have solved the case before him again . . . Yes, we will, and you can tell him that Daisy Wells says so . . . Don't you laugh at me! How rude! If you were my policeman I should demote you. Oh—Mummy's here. Bother. Tell Inspector Priestley—"

Lady Hastings wrenched the phone out of Daisy's grasp.

"Apologies, Inspector," she said breathlessly. "My daughter—oh. Who is this . . . ? Where is Inspector Priestley? Really, I do think we are being shoddily treated. Don't you know who I am . . . ? Yes, I know there are floods, but the rain is easing off now, and you ought to have been here hours ago! We've got a poor man's body simply *moldering* away upstairs, and we've been sent *no* support, and . . . Oh. You are coming? You'll be here tomorrow morning by boat? Well, I must say, it's not a moment too soon. What if there were to be another murder? I tell you, we are all in the most terrible danger . . . Yes . . . Yes . . . No, certainly not! . . . Yes . . . Oh, all right then. Good-bye."

She put down the phone with a clatter and sighed dramatically. She had an audience—and not just the two of us, either. While she was talking, the drawing room door had opened again, and Aunt Saskia's large face, all set about with earrings and scarves, had come poking out, a distinctly sharp and suspicious look on it under its puff of hair.

Robin Stevens

Behind her were Miss Alston and Uncle Felix (together again, I thought), and out of the library came Bertie, with Lord Hastings and Stephen behind him. All our suspects, in fact, were there, and they had all heard Lady Hastings's conversation. I saw Kitty and Beanie pop their heads round the door to the kitchens—even they were listening in.

"The police are on their way!" said Lady Hastings unnecessarily. "They think the flood will be down by morning now that the rain has stopped. We shall get to the bottom of this horrid business at last!"

"Mother, you are an idiot," said Bertie.

"I think what Bertie means," said Uncle Felix, "is that if you *do* get to the bottom of this, you might not like what you find."

"Oh, do be quiet, all of you!" cried Lady Hastings. "I know what you're trying to say, and I don't care! Denis has been *murdered*. I know you all hated him—he told me about the fearful argument you had with him, George, and about you threatening him, Felix. And his watch—*I* haven't seen it, have you, Saskia? Denis had no secrets from me, and I shan't hide anything from the police when they arrive tomorrow."

Aunt Saskia gasped. Miss Alston squeezed her lips tight shut, as though she were trying to stop words escaping. Bertie crumpled up his fist and slammed it into his open palm. "Come on, Stephen, don't just *stand* there," he said furiously. "I don't much feel like being in present company any longer."

Lord Hastings was standing stock-still in the library doorway, and he had turned a very funny puce color. His hands were clutched together over his bulging stomach and his mouth was open. "But, Margaret," he said, "you can't simply . . . Think of the *family*, Margaret . . ."

"Oh, family," said Lady Hastings rudely. "*Bother* family. Now, Chapman, stop gaping like a fool and go and see to dinner."

Everyone retreated upstairs—except Uncle Felix, who went toward the billiard room, and Miss Alston. She narrowed her eyes at us, tapped her wristwatch and said, "Almost time, girls. Be in the music room in *five minutes.*" Whether or not she was guilty, she was certainly menacing. "I must just get something from my room. Don't be late." She turned and went striding purposefully up the stairs, handbag swinging on her arm.

The air felt thick—or perhaps I was just not breathing very well. I couldn't do it, I thought in a panic. I couldn't behave as though everything was normal, when Miss Alston might have murdered Mr. Curtis—and might want to murder us all.

"Buck up, Watson!" whispered Daisy, and she squeezed my hand sharply. "She shan't hurt us! Detective Society forever!"

No matter how frightened I was, I couldn't let Daisy down. I took a deep breath and nodded.

"Kitty, Beanie!" called Daisy. "Time for lessons!"

Her voice didn't shake at all. Sometimes I think Daisy is quite marvelous.

Kitty and Beanie popped out of the kitchens, both looking as worried as I felt. Kitty seized hold of Beanie's arm and marched her forward, but before we were halfway across the hall Beanie gasped, "No! I won't! I don't want to!" and made a frantic dive for the library. We rushed after her, and found her huddled behind a sofa, whimpering.

"*Honestly,*" said Daisy.

We were still trying to decide what to do about her when the door opened again, and Bertie barged in.

"Hello!" he said, frowning. "Forgot something. What's all this then, Squashy?"

"Beanie's being silly," said Daisy, not looking at him. "Go *away,* Bertie—it's a girl thing."

"She's not upset about Mr. Curtis, is she?" asked Bertie. "You know there wasn't really a murder, don't you? Mummy's just being an idiot. Mind you, if someone *did* kill Curtis, we all ought to thank them."

"Stop it," snapped Daisy. "Don't be a fool. You're making yourself sound fearfully guilty."

Bertie glared at her for a moment, and I was afraid that he was going to do something awful, like shout, or strike her. But instead of that, he opened his mouth and roared with laughter.

"Squashy!" he howled. "What on earth—*me, guilty?* You

infernal little bungler! Why would I kill a cad like Curtis? He was mud on my shoe! I'd never . . . imagine risking the noose just to bump off Curtis!"

"But Mummy—," cried Daisy, her front quite down for a moment. "She and Mr. Curtis—"

"Mummy," said Bertie, "can do whatever she chooses. I gave up long ago, and if you had any sense, you would too. Daisy, if I was to bump off all Mummy's idiotic boyfriends, I'd be a murderer ten times over by now."

"That isn't true!" said Daisy. I put my hand on her arm. How awful. Poor Daisy!

"Of course it is," said Bertie. Footsteps came from the room above us, beating out his words terribly. "Don't you know anything?"

"You go away, Squinty, you awful beast!" Daisy shouted. "Don't you say that to me!"

And it was at that precise moment that we heard the most awful shriek from the second floor, and then a terrible thudding sound.

It hung in my ears like a blow. We stood still, and I counted ten beats of my heart in my head—the only noise in the whole silent house.

Then there was another shout. "HELP!" roared Uncle Felix's voice from the hall. "QUICK! HELP!"

"Oh, what is it?" cried Beanie, clutching at Kitty's sleeve.

"Don't ask!" said Daisy. "Hurry up! Something's *happened*!"

IX

W e raced out of the library, all five of us together. At the same time up popped Aunt Saskia at the turn of the stair, like a rabbit out of a hat, and then Lord Hastings came rushing down to join her, shouting, "Good Lord, what is it? What's happened?"

I heard Stephen come hammering down the main stairs from the nursery floor, and then he appeared too, looking plain terrified—I think the same look must have been on my face. There was an odd silence at the very middle of everything, something hot and terrible, like a fire covered over but still burning away.

Uncle Felix was kneeling in the middle of the hall, hunched over something piled up at the foot of the stairs. Miss Alston was standing behind him, very still. She was holding her handbag to her chest with both hands pressed together in front of her, so tightly that they looked like twisted vines. I wondered what would make her hold herself like that. But she was only staring at the bundle of clothes in front of Uncle Felix. His shouts must simply have been a mistake.

I felt dreadfully relieved.

Then the clothes moved.

It seemed as though the whole house gasped, but really I think it was only me. Aunt Saskia screamed, "MARGARET!" which sounded terribly false and out of place, and made my ears hurt.

"Good Lord," said Lord Hastings emptily. "Good Lord! What's happened!"

"Margaret's fallen down the stairs," said Uncle Felix. "She's badly hurt. She needs a doctor—quick!"

He looked at Miss Alston, but it was Bertie who answered. "I'll call!" he snapped. "She's *my* mother."

The door from the kitchens opened, and Chapman came out. "What's happened?" he cried. He saw Lady Hastings lying on the floor, and went quite gray with horror. He began to look up, toward where Lord Hastings was standing, but then he dragged his gaze back down with a jolt.

Daisy surged forward, but Uncle Felix held his hands out against her like a shield. "No!" he said. "Don't look."

"Really!" said Daisy. "Am I allowed to do anything this weekend?"

"Daisy!" said Uncle Felix fiercely.

"Oh, all right!" said Daisy, a shrill note in her voice. "If you're going to be a *grown-up* about it."

I put my arm round her as Bertie shouted for the operator to get him Dr. Cooper *at once*, and Aunt Saskia swayed and wailed, clinging to Lord Hastings. I could feel Daisy shivering as though she had a fever.

Uncle Felix was kneeling over the bundle that was Lady Hastings, while Miss Alston spoke short, quiet words in his ear. Once again they were behaving as though they knew each other very well. I thought of what Uncle Felix had said a few minutes ago—*Margaret's fallen down the stairs*. I couldn't believe that. Someone must have pushed her. Uncle Felix seemed to be helping her now, but he had arrived on the scene awfully quickly—and so had Miss Alston. What had she gone to collect, after all? Had it been a ruse to get us out of the way for a moment?

Then I looked up at the main stairs. They were dark and twisting and shadowy—the day had faded, and the electric lamps had not yet been put on. It was just the place for an ambush. Someone must have pushed Lady Hastings down from the very top—exactly where Aunt Saskia and Lord Hastings had come from. Once again, I thought with a feeling of hopelessness, Lord Hastings *seemed* very suspicious. I believed Daisy—I *did*, I told myself firmly—but the police wouldn't. The only thing that made me feel even the smallest bit glad was that, at last, we had ruled out one of Daisy's family. Bertie had been with us the moment we heard Lady Hastings scream—there was no possible way, even with the most cunning of plans, that he could have been the person who pushed her.

X

We were banished to the drawing room, with the door shut and a box of dominoes in front of us. Toast Dog and Millie were there too, whining and grumbling and aching to be let out. None of us quite knew what to do with them—or ourselves.

Beanie was crying. "Your poor mummy!" she wailed. "Will she be all right? Will she?"

"I don't know!" said Daisy ferociously. She had posted herself just inside the closed door, and was listening to the noises outside. Toast Dog waddled over to stand beside her, and it was almost funny to see how alike they looked— golden and hopeful, ears pricked. "Can't you be quiet for a bit? I want to think."

"I'm sure she will be," said Kitty, trying to be helpful. "My aunt knows someone who fell from the very top of a block of flats—all the way down the stairs—and she lived. She broke every bone in her body, of course, and she walked very oddly afterward, but—"

"Kitty," I said. "Be quiet."

Kitty closed her mouth, scowling. "Rude," she muttered to herself.

For a moment Beanie was quiet too. Then she said, "D'you think the police really will be here tomorrow?"

"Ha!" said Daisy. "What can they do? I hope they never come at all. They'll only ruin everything." I knew she was thinking about Lord Hastings.

"But if the police don't come," said Beanie nervously, "how will we stop the murderer? I know you say the police can't help, but won't they protect us? Two people have been hurt now!"

"Daisy," I said, because I had to, "she is right. We want the police to come, don't we? And it's Inspector Priestley. Remember Deepdean? He's clever. He'll know it isn't your father!"

"Will he?" asked Daisy.

Outside, the front door slammed, and we heard a new voice, tidy and carrying. Dr. Cooper had arrived. The dogs went wild, and Toast Dog flung himself quite heavily against the closed door.

"He may be a nice clodhopper, but he's still a clodhopper. He's got to stick to the rules."

"But if he catches the real murderer—" said Kitty.

"He may not!" snapped Daisy. "And anyway, we'll be perfectly all right. We must just stick together—and bar the door to the nursery before we go to bed tonight. They can't kill all four of us."

As usual when Daisy tries to reassure people, this was not at all comforting. Beanie wailed, and I silently agreed with her. If the murderer was going to strike again, we were surely next. How could we think we were safe? Even if we ran, we would be brought back—within easy reach of the murderer.

I imagined Inspector Priestley wading through the receding floods toward us, his greatcoat swishing behind him, and willed him to hurry up. For all that Daisy did not trust the police, he had saved us once before—and now, I felt, it was time for him to do so again. I wanted to get away from Fallingford and never come back. I missed my Hong Kong home, where everything was hot and light and safe. And despite what had happened there last year, I missed Deepdean. I felt a rush of remembering it—for a moment I thought I could almost smell it, chalk and not-clean socks and cold water. It washed over my memory of home, which was only very faint now, like my mother's perfume on my clothes. I wasn't sure which place I wanted more.

Daisy was still talking, faster and faster, a river of sound that I struggled to make sense of: ". . . but we must be vigilant. As soon as we're let out of this silly room we must remember to check our suspects' alibis for the time Mummy was pushed. Pay attention to everything—not just what they say, but how they say it. Modern detectives need to be psychological, because you see, today's criminal mind is cleverer than ever—it says so in my books—and—"

But just then she was interrupted by the most dreadful noise. It was a groaning; a horrible howl that started very low down and rose up through the scale, so that it seemed to go twisting up my spine in coils.

"Ugh!" cried Kitty. "What's that?"

"Oh!" wailed Beanie. "Is she dead? What's wrong? Oh dear!"

Daisy's head jerked up and her eyes went wide.

"What is it?" I asked her. I was very afraid of the answer.

Daisy took a deep breath. "That," she said composedly, "is Mummy. It's the noise she makes when she thinks she's dreadfully hurt—generally after she's bumped her elbow. And if she's making it now, it means that she's going to be all right. She's not going to die after all—not that I ever thought she would. And if you'll all excuse me for one moment, I must just . . ."

And she got up from her chair, walked carefully over to the ornamental plant on the sideboard and very neatly threw up into the pot.

Part Five
But Who Else Is Left?

O h, it was dreadful," said Lady Hastings. She was lying on a sofa in the library, her head swaddled in a pillowy white bandage and one arm strapped to her chest. The rest of us were gathered round her like an audience.

Before we were let out of the drawing room, we had managed to overhear Dr. Cooper talking to Uncle Felix in the hall. Apparently it was a wonder that Lady Hastings wasn't more severely injured. "She must have hit her head on the banister as she went down," he said (rather crossly, as though Lady Hastings had no right to her good fortune). "She was concussed, and that made her go limp and roll. Most falling cases try to stop themselves, and that's when the damage is done. All I can find here is a fracture of the ulna, and extensive bruising. And the concussion, of course. She'll have to be watched closely. How did it happen?"

"Carelessness," said Uncle Felix briefly. (*Lying again!* I

thought. He must surely know that this was no more an accident than Mr. Curtis's death!) "My sister is a liability. Now, please don't worry yourself—we shall take very good care of her."

"Oh no," said Dr. Cooper. "She needs expert care—at least for tonight. I'll stay here at Fallingford and sit with her. None of us would forgive ourselves if anything happened to dear Lady Hastings, would we?"

"Indeed not," said Uncle Felix blandly. "Thank you, Doctor. And—have you had a chance to send off those samples yet?"

"Not yet," Dr. Cooper replied. "As soon as the floods have gone, I shall, I assure you. You've called the police—for the body?"

"They're on their way," said Uncle Felix—and again, his voice gave nothing away.

At last we were released—and made straight for Lady Hastings and the other grown-ups in the library. As Daisy had said, we had to collect alibis as quickly as possible—but for a while we learned absolutely nothing of interest. It was very frustrating. All Lady Hastings did was complain very loudly about her headache. "Is there a cut on my forehead?" she asked anxiously. "Imagine if I'm scarred! Oh, and my arm! I might never play the piano again!"

"Don't talk, Lady Hastings," said Miss Alston. "Just rest."

I flinched. Given what we had discovered about her,

everything Miss Alston said seemed menacing. Her presence in the room made my back hot, as though her eyes were on it. Did she know that we suspected her? Meanwhile Daisy was watching the handbag like a mongoose after a snake. A few times I had to nudge her to stop her being so obvious. "She must put it down!" she whispered in my ear. "She *must!*" But Miss Alston never did.

"How can I rest?" cried Lady Hastings. "The most dreadful things have happened to me. I was pushed!"

Miss Alston made a vague noise, and Uncle Felix raised his eyebrow. There they were again, I thought in frustration, pretending that everything sinister was imagined.

"It's true!" said Lady Hastings indignantly. "Every time I close my eyes I feel it all over again. Those shadowy stairs—the silence—and then those terrible hands, shoving me in the back—so cruel! I remember thinking, *This is the end!* And then something hit my head and there was nothing more. I thought I had *died!*"

"Incredible," murmured Bertie. "Thinking while unconscious."

"Do be quiet, thankless child," snapped his mother. "But what I want to know now is, who is responsible for what happened to me?"

"What do you mean?" twittered Aunt Saskia. She was pretending ignorance too, although not as well as Miss Alston or Uncle Felix.

"Exactly what I said. I was not attacked by a ghost, now, was I? Someone *did* that to me. Someone in this house! Only imagine . . . what cruelty, what meanness—what have I ever done to deserve it?"

"That," said Bertie, "is perhaps not a question you would like us to answer honestly."

Lady Hastings ignored him.

"I assure you, Margaret, I had nothing to do with it," said Aunt Saskia.

Daisy sat up and poked me. Were we about to hear an alibi?

"I was in my bedchamber . . . reading, yes, reading a lovely book, when I heard your terrible scream. I rushed out of the room and met dear George, who was already on the landing—we rushed downstairs and saw Felix kneeling over your lifeless body. Or so I thought. Of course, I was *dreadfully* glad that it wasn't, you know, truly lifeless after all. George, don't you remember?" She patted down the front of her dress, rearranging her scarves, and as she did so she gave off a waft of ghostly smell that made my nose wrinkle. Beneath her own sickly sweet bluebell scent was something else; something dirty and unpleasant. I could almost taste it. Whatever could it be?

Lord Hastings did a funny sort of wriggle. "I . . . ," he said. "I . . . er, yes, I must have done. I came out of my room, I saw you, I . . . Yes, that's it. That's what happened."

Robin Stevens

I saw Daisy give him a worried glance. What was he playing at this time? It sounded like another lie.

"I was also in my room," said Miss Alston, "fetching a book for the girls' lesson. I ran out at once, and saw no one else in the hall."

"And I was in the billiard room," said Uncle Felix shortly.

I thought of something very odd, then. If the servants had been in the kitchens, and everyone else had been in their own rooms, except for Uncle Felix (who had been down on the first floor—or at least, so he said), Stephen (up on the nursery floor), and Lady Hastings (who had been standing at the top of the stairs, about to be pushed off them by the murderer), then who had I heard walking above us while we were in the library, just before Lady Hastings screamed and fell? The room above the library was Mr. Curtis's, I realized now. And Mr. Curtis's room, we all knew, was locked. I felt a creepy sensation go up my back. I didn't believe in ghosts anymore, I told myself. I was far too grown-up. But all the same . . .

I imagined clicking open Mr. Curtis's door and creeping into that dark room—I wondered if it smelled. I wondered if the shadows were tall and creeping. I wondered whether Mr. Curtis's body was still lying on the bed.

"Yes, but this doesn't help *me*," said Lady Hastings crossly. "We don't know who pushed me down the stairs, and until we do I'm quite sure that I won't be able to sleep.

Just think, the attacker might come back! I demand a guard at all times!"

"Dr. Cooper will be here," said Uncle Felix. "And so will the rest of us."

"But it was one of you who did THIS!" shouted Lady Hastings. "Who else could it have been? I didn't hear the dogs bark, did you? There's been no one else in this house all weekend."

Beanie, of course, burst into tears.

"Margaret!" said Lord Hastings, looking at her awkwardly. "The children!"

"I think that *some people* ought to go upstairs," said Miss Alston, clearing her throat. "I shall have your dinner brought up."

"But we want to stay with Mummy," said Daisy loudly. I grasped her hand and squeezed it. At that moment I could not decide what would be worse—being stuck upstairs in the dark nursery with Miss Alston next door, or being downstairs with Lady Hastings, knowing that the murderer might come back to finish her off at any moment.

"Don't be silly, Daisy dear," said Aunt Saskia, drawing herself up with all her earrings jingling and wrapping her nasty flat-faced fur stole around her neck. "Grown-ups know what's best for little people. And I confess, I find myself quite tired as well. I shall take a little something from the kitchens and retire to my bedchamber—and I

Robin Stevens

shall lock the door. The murderer shan't be able to get in!"

She spun about on her flat old-lady heels. Her dress billowed out—and something fell tinkling out of it onto the floor. Quick as a flash, Daisy put her foot on it, and then stared up at the ceiling most innocently.

Aunt Saskia froze. I could tell that she was desperate to bend down and snatch up whatever had fallen—though at the very same time, she knew she mustn't. She paused in the doorway, twisting her fingers up into her scarves . . . and then the part of her that couldn't afford to make a fuss won.

"Oh—good night!" she gasped, and trotted out into the hallway, shoulders all hunched up and hands clenched. It had obviously cost her to leave without whatever it was. I tingled all over with curiosity.

"Oh!" I said, as though I had made an interesting discovery. "My shoe is untied." I bent down, and under cover of fiddling with my left lace I slid my hand next to Daisy's shoe. She wiggled it aside obligingly, and my fingers closed around something metal-cold and knobbly. What it felt like was a key.

"There!" I said, standing up again and palming the key into the sleeve of my cardigan. "Done."

Daisy pinched me appreciatively.

"All right then, girls," said Miss Alston severely. "Bed."

"Oh, Miss Alston," said Daisy. "Must we?"

"You must," said Miss Alston, folding her arms across her

chest. "I shall be up in ten minutes to make sure you have your nighties on—and if you do, then I will send Hetty up with dinner."

Ordinarily, this would have been enough to cheer me up, but given the circumstances, it sounded most menacing. What if Miss Alston should slip something into the cocoa? There had been one poisoning already, after all.

I wanted to stay downstairs, in the light and warmth of the library, and I could tell the others did too. But with all the grown-ups watching us, we had no choice but to shuffle out of the room and upstairs.

Robin Stevens

W e walked up through the dim and dusty house, keeping very close together. After all that had just happened—and my thoughts about the dinner—my heart was racing. What was the key I had just picked up? Which door would it open? I unfolded my hand and stared at it, and quick as a flash Daisy poked her nose over my shoulder and said, "Key!"

"Ooh," said Kitty, staring too. "What does it open?"

As soon as she asked, I *knew*.

We were on the second-floor landing, about to take the main stairs up to the nursery floor. The lamps were on now, but the bulbs were dim and flickering, and in the odd half-light the house looked very chilly and uncertain. I wasn't surprised that someone could have crept up behind Lady Hastings in the five o'clock half dark— even now I could barely make out the others around me. I held out the key.

"Is it . . . the key to the dining room?" whispered Beanie. "Oh no, Aunt Saskia did it!"

"Don't be silly," said Daisy. "We told you, the murderer would have put that key back straight afterward. Uncle Felix hasn't squeaked about it, after all. No, this is something quite different."

"Exactly!" I said. "It is! If I'm right, I mean."

"You usually are," said Daisy. "Apart from when I am, of course. So, Watson, what door do you think this key opens?"

I took a deep breath. "Mr. Curtis's," I said.

Daisy raised one eyebrow (her practice must have paid off). "*Explain*," she said.

"We know Aunt Saskia likes to, um, pick up beautiful things," I said. "And we all saw how she was staring at the watch earlier this weekend. We've been hunting for the watch all day—what if she has too? She must have guessed that Mr. Curtis took it upstairs with him when he was taken ill—although *we* know he didn't—and that it would still be in his room. So she took this key from the bunch in the kitchens sometime this afternoon and went into Mr. Curtis's room to look for it. Just before Lady Hastings fell I heard footsteps above us in the library. I couldn't work out how someone could be in Mr. Curtis's room—but if it was Aunt Saskia, looking for the watch, then everything makes sense."

"But if she was looking for the watch just now, she couldn't have been the person who took it from the dining room on Saturday night!" said Kitty. "And if we heard her footsteps in Mr. Curtis's room just as Lady Hastings was being pushed—well, she couldn't have been the person to push her. She *can't* be the murderer!"

"Very true!" said Daisy. "Excellent work, Assistant Kitty!"

"Ugh," Kitty added, wrinkling up her nose. "Just imagine. She went into a room with a dead body."

I remembered the nasty smell that had drifted off Aunt Saskia's clothes.

"So?" said Daisy. I do wonder about her sometimes. She is quite odd in the way she reacts to things. "It's just a dead body. It can't bite. Hazel, hand me that key. Your theory is very good, and I don't doubt it's right, but there's a way to make quite sure—we need to check that this key really *does* open the door to Mr. Curtis's room."

"Ugh!" said Kitty again.

"No!" cried Beanie.

"But," I said, "Daisy, the *body*." Mr. Curtis might not be a ghost, but he had been dead for quite some time.

"Huh," she said. "*Key*, Hazel."

I handed it to her, and we all three watched as Daisy went up to Mr. Curtis's door.

"She's very brave," said Beanie.

"She's quite mad," muttered Kitty. "Goodness, I never knew."

But as I stood there, I understood, just a little, what Daisy meant about the body. It couldn't hurt us. Nothing on the other side of that door could be as terrible as the murderer. Daisy was doing something nasty to make sure we were all safe.

As Beanie protested, and Kitty looked on breathlessly, I stayed quiet—and Daisy put the key into the lock and clicked open Mr. Curtis's door.

A horrid, thin smell came wafting through the crack, making me gulp. It was exactly what I had smelled on Aunt Saskia before.

I was right. Aunt Saskia *had* been in this room at the moment when Lady Hastings had screamed. She couldn't have pushed her off the top of the stairs—and so she couldn't be Mr. Curtis's murderer.

D aisy pulled Mr. Curtis's door closed again and locked it. "What we need to do," she said, slipping the key into her pocket, "is hold another Detective Society meeting before dinner. This won't end unless *we* end it, don't you see? The murderer won't stop. And they've hurt my mother. She may be a silly mother, but she is *mine*, and I won't have it! I'm going to *do* something, and you're all going to help me. All right?"

I nodded. "All right," I said. I knew I was bound to help Daisy all the way to the end.

"All right," said Kitty, glancing at Beanie and then back at us. "We're in too."

We climbed the stairs to the nursery and then sat in a circle on the old rag rug in the middle of the room. Daisy had set a candle in its old brass holder between us, and it lit us all softly, shadows flickering across our faces. It felt lovely, but creepy at the same time. I had my casebook on my lap, and Daisy, of course, was leading the meeting. If there *had* been a table, she would have been at the head. Beanie kept fidgeting and staring at the closed nursery door. I knew Daisy was fearfully annoyed by her—but it was terribly difficult not to be as wobbly as Beanie. I felt as though the mystery were rushing to its conclusion, and we were being rushed along with it. Would we get to the truth before the police arrived—or before the murderer got to *us*?

"All right," Daisy said. "This meeting of the Detective Society is hereby called to attention. Present are myself, Hazel, Kitty, and Beanie—write it all down, Hazel, you know what to do by now.

"The facts of the case are these. At just after five p.m. (we know the time, because Miss Alston had just called us for that five o'clock lesson she'd been threatening) someone pushed Mummy down the stairs. From her account we know that it happened—she isn't so silly that she can't tell when someone is pushing her—but that she didn't see who did it. The top of the stairs was dark, and whoever it was came up behind her and shoved. Hazel, write all that down.

"Now, this new crime was of course awful for Mummy, but it does finally give us the evidence we need to absolutely rule out some of our suspects."

"Bertie," I said, scribbling.

"Exactly! We can give Bertie an absolutely watertight alibi. He was with us when we heard Mummy fall—there simply isn't any way that he could have pushed her down the stairs unless he has magical powers, and I know for a fact that he doesn't. Of course, whoever hurt Mummy might not necessarily be the person who killed Mr. Curtis—but really, it's quite impossible to believe that there are *two* murderers running about the house. So I think it's safe to assume that they are one and the same. And that means that Bertie simply couldn't have done the poisoning."

I crossed through Bertie's name gladly.

"And if we wondered about Mummy before, she is quite obviously out of the picture now. I'm sure there are some people in the world who would throw themselves down the stairs to make them appear innocent of a previous crime, but Mummy isn't one of them. She absolutely hates being hurt, and she's always terribly worried about becoming ugly. So she's out too.

"Next is Aunt Saskia. Hazel very cleverly used the key she dropped to rule her out of shoving Mummy—well done, Hazel, top detective-ing—so although we know that she's got dreadfully sticky fingers, we can be sure that she is also innocent of Mr. Curtis's murder."

I crossed out busily. "And, Daisy, we heard Stephen come running down from the third floor just after the push. If you add that to what I told you about him being on a scholarship, you have to admit that it's not just me sticking up for him because he's nice. He *can't* be a suspect."

I could feel my cheeks growing hot again—which was silly. I was only being logical.

Kitty grinned at me (I looked away), but Daisy nodded. "Yes, all right," she said. "We've got rid of Stephen's motive for the first crime, and his opportunity for the second, so we can take him off the list. That means we're down to three. Miss Alston, Uncle Felix . . . and Daddy."

"But didn't you tell us that we shouldn't suspect your father?" Kitty asked.

"Yes, and I also told you that the clodhoppers wouldn't understand that at all. They're such sillies, they won't listen to us without real evidence. So we must give it to them."

"But if he loves your mother, why would he try to hurt her?" asked Beanie, eyes wide.

"Exactly!" said Daisy. "Excellent point, Assistant Beanie. If Daddy wanted Mummy back so badly that he was willing to kill Mr. Curtis, then why would he push Mummy off the stairs? But the police might think he was cross with Mummy and wanted to punish her—so even that doesn't let him off."

We all sighed.

"And we *did* see him standing on the landing with Aunt Saskia afterward," I said.

"I know. Bother! He keeps on managing to make himself look so guilty! He's already got Chapman covering for him because of something that happened at tea yesterday, and

Robin Stevens

now this. Knowing Daddy—and I *do* know Daddy—there's something else in his head, but to an outsider he looks like the absolute perfect suspect. If we don't help him, he'll end up being arrested and thrown in jail. Poor Daddy, Parliament will be furious with him. He'll have to go on trial—oh, it'll be just like the poor stupid Duke of Denver in that book. And then . . ." Daisy paused. She was sunk in gloom, and we all understood why. If Lord Hastings was thrown in jail and put on trial, and if there was no evidence that he was innocent—he would be found guilty, and then nothing could save him.

"But what about Miss Alston and Uncle Felix?" I asked, to divert her thoughts. "They weren't just on the stairs when we came out of the library; they were *next* to your mother. Miss Alston said that when she went out onto the second-floor landing there was no one else there—and there wouldn't be, if *she* was the one who'd pushed Lady Hastings."

"And your uncle Felix *was* being suspicious again," put in Kitty. I could tell that she'd had the same idea as me. "He didn't want anyone else touching your mother."

Daisy frowned. "Uncle Felix was probably trying to look after her," she said. "She *is* his sister, after all. But I admit, when added to his other behavior this weekend, it is concerning. Oh, I don't like it! It doesn't seem . . . How would Uncle Felix know someone like Miss Alston? We know she's lying about who she is and what she's doing here! Oh, I wish we could get into her handbag and discover what it is she's hiding! But how are we to do that? We don't have much time—the police will be here terribly soon, and we must be able to lead them to the murderer as soon as they arrive."

"We could ask her for it," said Beanie.

"Beanie, really, be sensible. If she's the murderer, she's not likely to agree, is she? In fact, that's just the sort of idea that's likely to end with us getting bumped off. Try again."

"We could all scream that there's a fire, and hope that she drops it?" suggested Kitty.

Daisy glared, and the meeting disintegrated into a rather loud argument.

SUSPECT LIST

Miss Alston. MOTIVE: Unknown. But we suspect that she has some sort of secret history which Mr. Curtis knew about. OPPORTUNITY: Was at the tea table at the crucial time. Could have stolen the poison from the hall. NOTES: Was seen being threatened by Mr. Curtis outside the maze by Daisy Wells and Hazel Wong. Was seen hiding a piece of paper suspiciously. Who is she really, and what is she doing here? We know that her letters of reference are false.

Aunt Saskia. MOTIVE: Wanted Mr. Curtis's watch. OPPORTUNITY: Was at the tea table at the crucial time. Could have stolen the poison from the hall. NOTES: Has been behaving suspiciously. Does not want the police to get involved although this could be because of other misdemeanours in her past. Search her room for the watch? RULED OUT! She was in Mr. Curtis's room—looking for the watch, we believe—when Lady Hastings was attacked.

Uncle Felix. MOTIVE: Rage at Mr. Curtis over Lady Hastings. He was heard in the maze threatening Mr. Curtis by Daisy Wells and Hazel Wong. OPPORTUNITY: Was at the tea table at the crucial time. Could have stolen the poison from the hall. NOTES: We know he has lied about Mr. Curtis's cause of death. Why?

Lord Hastings. MOTIVE: Jealousy. OPPORTUNITY: Was at the tea table at the crucial time. Could have stolen the poison from the hall. NOTES: Seen shouting at Mr. Curtis on Saturday morning and telling him to leave Fallingford. Seen handing Mr. Curtis's cup to him at Saturday's tea. The return of the teacup proves to the Detective Society that Lord Hastings is not the murderer, but we will need more concrete evidence to convince the police. Chapman appears to be covering for him for some reason. Was seen after the second crime at the turn of the stairs—in the right place at the right time to be the murderer.

Bertie Wells. MOTIVE: ~~Rage at Mr. Curtis over Lady Hastings.~~ OPPORTUNITY: ~~Was at the tea table at the crucial time. Could have stolen the poison from the hall.~~ *RULED OUT!* He was with the Detective Society at the moment Lady Hastings was attacked.

Stephen Bampton. MOTIVE: ~~He is not well-off. Could he have stolen Mr. Curtis's watch to sell it?~~ OPPORTUNITY: ~~Was at the tea table at the crucial time. Could have stolen the poison from the hall.~~ *RULED OUT:* He does not need money—he has a full scholarship to Eton and then to Cambridge, so he has no motive for the crimes. We also heard him coming down from the nursery floor just after Lady Hastings was pushed down the stairs.

Lady Hastings. MOTIVE: ~~Mr. Curtis threatened her. She might have killed him to stop him carrying out his threat.~~ OPPORTUNITY: ~~Was at the tea table at the crucial time. Could have stolen the poison from the hall.~~ *RULED OUT:* She was the victim of the second attack.

Robin Stevens

I left them to it and went to the bathroom to get a drink.
And there was someone on the landing.

A dark shape was lurking in the shadows next to the window at the front of the house. My heart stumbled, and I gasped, backing away toward the nursery door. I wanted to scream, but just as in my nightmares, I couldn't make any sound at all. The murderer was here and was about to catch me alone.

The shape shook itself loose of the shadows and came creeping toward me. "Hazel," said Stephen's quiet voice. "Hazel, stop! It's me!"

My voice came back with a gasp. "What are you doing there?" I said. "You—I thought you were—"

"Terribly sorry," said Stephen. "I didn't mean to upset you. I only wanted to find a place to think."

Trying to quiet my heart, I went to stand next to him at the window. It is a lovely round one, like a porthole in the sky, and ivy wiggles across it like thin fingers. You can see the drive, and some of the monkey-puzzle tree. Outside, the rain really had eased up, and there was a thin glaze of moonlight over everything that made the monkey-puzzle look as if it had been cut out with scissors.

"Are you all right?" Stephen asked me quietly.

"Yes," I whispered back. "I suppose so. Are you?"

"Sometimes I don't feel as if I shall ever be all right again," said Stephen.

I wanted to say that this was exactly what I had been feeling too, without being able to explain it.

"I wish this was all over," I said miserably.

"I wish it had never begun," said Stephen, scowling. He rested his forehead against the windowpane and shivered. When he leaned back again, his hair was damp and sticking up, and there was a little drop of water curling down his cheek.

"My father left us," he said quietly. "Did you know that? This weekend—it's brought it all back. It feels like it only happened yesterday. It feels like it's still happening."

I didn't know what to say. I stared out at the tree, and noticed that it made angles in the shadow on the drive; that I could see every single funny leaf. "I feel like that sometimes too," I said at last. "Last year, a mistress at our school . . . died, and I found her. I *touched* her. It . . . wasn't very nice. Daisy thinks I should forget about it, but I can't, somehow."

It was Stephen's turn to nod.

"I'm sorry about your father," I said.

"Thank you. Listen, Hazel. You mustn't worry. What I mean to say is, you're quite safe. Bertie and I—we won't let anything happen to the four of you. I can promise that."

He paused, and I paused too, looking at him. Everything seemed frozen—until a little gust of wind shook the panes in front of us and made us start.

"And the police are coming," I said. "Inspector Priestley will help us."

I hoped I was right.

It was only after I was back in the nursery that I realized I had forgotten to get that drink. Daisy, Kitty, and Beanie were still talking, so I sat up in bed and began to write in this casebook. When there was a knock on the nursery door I nearly jumped out of my skin—but it was only Mrs. Doherty, coming up with the dinner. It was egg and toast again—and a jelly roll.

We must be very close indeed to solving the crime now—but all the same, I'm still not sure that this is a case that the Detective Society ought to solve. There seems to be something lying just out of reach, waiting for us.

Part Six
The Detective Society Solves the Case

On Monday morning I woke up with a jolt, and found that I was still clinging to this casebook, and that my pencil had got loose and gone in scribbling snail trails across my bedsheets.

Daisy was shaking my arm, and in my ear the house's pipes were singing and shaking the bed as someone ran a bath in the nursery bathroom.

"Hazel!" Daisy was saying. "Hazel! Hazel! HAZEL, WAKE UP!"

"I'm awake," I said. "*Ow.*"

"Hazel, a miracle has happened. Miss Alston is taking a bath."

I couldn't quite see how this was a miracle. Miss Alston was not a particularly dirty person.

"Hazel, don't be slow. What don't people take into bathrooms, even if they carry them everywhere else? What is liable to get all steamed up and unpleasant if it sits next to a hot bath?"

I suddenly saw what she was getting at. "A handbag!"

"Indeed, Watson. Indeed!"

We beamed at each other.

"Up! We must work quickly," said Daisy. "Kitty, I want you standing outside the bathroom, listening for movement. Beanie, you can stand guard just outside Miss Alston's room, to whisper to us if Kitty gives the alarm, and, Hazel, you come into the room with me."

"But I want—" Kitty began.

"No arguing!" cried Daisy. "I am the Detective Society president, and in this case you must respect my authority, because I know what I am talking about and I solved a real murder case last year. With Hazel. All right. Are you ready?"

Kitty and Beanie nodded—although Kitty's nod was slightly reluctant.

"Excellent," said Daisy. "Ready, Watson?"

"Ready," I said. And we crept out of the nursery doorway onto the upstairs landing.

The noise from the pipes stopped as Kitty positioned herself outside the bathroom and Beanie stood nervously just outside Miss Alston's door. Daisy and I gave the Detective Society handshake once, for luck, and then Daisy pushed open Miss Alston's door. We were inside again.

Robin Stevens

The bed was made. The drawers were closed. And Miss Alston's brown handbag was sitting plumply on her pillow.

"View-halloo, Watson!" hissed Daisy, eyes shining. "I knew we'd get it in the end. I knew it!" She leaped toward it like a cat.

"Careful!" I said. "You'll spill it—she mustn't know we've been here!"

"Ha," said Daisy. "There's no time for that."

In one movement, she spun the handbag upside down, and everything inside it tumbled out across the covers. It was as though Miss Alston had pinched her bag from Mary Poppins. Out came ruled paper and notebooks and cookies and maps and a compass and a bar of Fry's chocolate and a packet of pins and a needle and thread—and a bit of paper. It was the paper we had seen Miss Alston hiding, all that time ago in the music room!

Potential targets, it read. *Jeweled bracelet. Ming vase. Old master painting.*

My brain whirled. Was Miss Alston a thief, just like Mr. Curtis? Then I saw something beneath the paper, something flat and spiky, made of silver that glinted up at us.

"What's that?" I whispered, and "What's THIS?" hissed Daisy, and she picked it up and peered at it. Then she dropped it as though it had burned her. "Hazel," she said. "You won't believe this. *Look.*"

I looked. The silver thing was a badge, small enough to

fit in the palm of my hand. It had a little silver crest at the top: METROPOLITAN POLICE, it read.

"But—how did she get this?" I asked. "It's a *police* badge!"

"Do you think she *stole* it?" asked Daisy. "Gosh, what with this and that list, what if she's *actually* a criminal, just like Mr. Curtis was? Oh, we've got evidence at last! Miss Alston stole from a police officer—ha! And here, under all that, are the papers that I do believe will finally incriminate her!" Out of the bottom of the bag, with a flourish, she pulled a crumpled letter.

"It's from the police!" cried Daisy. "Look at that official letterhead! And it says—"

I bent over her and read. "*Oh*," I said.

Daisy and I stared at each other in utter shock.

Dear Miss Livedon,

You have been assigned to an undercover post at Fallingford House, home of Lord and Lady Hastings. You will pose as governess to their young but not-at-all impressionable daughter, Daisy Wells, and secretary to Lord Hastings, and you are asked to watch the movements of Mr. Denis Curtis, who will be arriving as a guest of Lady Hastings at an upcoming weekend party. Curtis is a notorious thief whose method seems to be to ingratiate himself with the lady of a large country house in order to gain access to the house's

Robin Stevens

contents. After a brief visit he leaves, and several priceless artifacts, usually including jewels, leave with him. We need you to catch him at it, to be blunt.

You have been furnished with the appropriate references, but Lord Hastings is of a trusting disposition, and so you are not likely to be grilled on your life story. Nevertheless, the daughter is another matter, and so it would be advisable to be on your guard around her. The name on your letters of reference is Miss Lucy Alston.

I wish you good luck, and will, of course, deny all knowledge of you if pressed.

M.

"Young but not at all impressionable!" gasped Daisy. "Hazel, look, I told you I was famous."

I felt that she was rather missing the point. "But now we know who Miss Alston really is!" I said. "This is the secret she's been hiding. She didn't steal from the police, she's one of them!"

"Oh yes!" said Daisy, coming back to earth.

We gaped at each other. Miss Alston a policewoman! She had been watching Mr. Curtis because she had been sent to catch him. That was why she had been acting so suspiciously, and why Mr. Curtis had threatened her on Saturday morning. He must have realized that she was after him, and tried to bluster to frighten her away. It was exactly the sort of arrogant thing that Mr. Curtis *would* do. And of course, Miss Alston—Livedon—must have begun her own investigation into Mr. Curtis's death. She must have taken his notebook from his room, and then dropped it—that was why we had found it on the floor. When we overheard her speaking to Stephen, she had not been threatening him, she had been trying to interrogate him, to find out what he knew about the murder!

"Well!" said Daisy. "I said she was too clever to simply be a governess. Oh golly, imagine—we've been taught by a policewoman. An undercover one! *Hazel!*"

Then I had a thought that wriggled uncomfortably at the bottom of my stomach. "But if she's a policewoman, Daisy, she can't be the murderer. You aren't allowed to murder people, are you, even when you're on undercover missions?"

"But—," Daisy began.

"Daisy!" whispered Beanie, outside. "Daisy! Hazel! Kitty says *she's getting out!*"

Quick as a flash, Daisy piled everything back into the handbag. It went in higgledy-piggledy, and I was only glad that it had been in such a mess in the first place. Miss Alston—Miss Livedon—might never know it had been searched. Daisy seized my hand and we scuttled out. Beanie

Robin Stevens

was bouncing up and down in an agony of fear, while Kitty stood with her hands pressed to her mouth. She let out a rush of breath when she saw us. "I thought you'd never come out!" she hissed.

The bathroom door opened, and Miss Alston emerged, hair damp and wearing a robe. She looked around at us all—at Beanie, trembling, at Kitty, all red in the face, and at Daisy and me, both trying desperately not to look at her bedroom door. Had we closed it properly?

"What are you doing here?" she asked. "Hurry downstairs to breakfast at once. Beanie, I think your father *will* be able to come for you and Kitty today." And she swept into her bedroom and shut the door behind her.

"Come on!" cried Daisy, and she went rattling down the main stairs like a dynamo.

"What did you find?" gasped Kitty as we dashed along behind her. "What happened?"

"Miss Alston is a *policewoman*!" I said. "On a secret mission to catch Mr. Curtis! She can't have done the murders!"

"But . . . ," said Kitty. "If she's a policewoman—there are only two suspects left!"

"I know," I said, and my heart sank horribly. "Uncle Felix . . . and Daisy's father."

D aisy stopped on the second-floor landing. "Aren't we going to breakfast?" I asked, because even though exciting things were going on all around me, I couldn't stop my stomach wanting toast and marmalade.

"NO!" said Daisy loudly. "The police will be here any minute. We must speak to Chapman again quickly, and make him tell us what he's hiding."

Chapman was tidying Uncle Felix's room, and he looked up as we went in.

"Miss Daisy!" he said. "Girls! What are you doing here?"

"There's no time for that," said Daisy. "We've got something we need to ask you. It's *important*! We heard you speaking to Daddy yesterday—we know what he said to you. You saw something—something he did at Saturday tea—and now he's making you keep quiet about it because he thinks it'll get him into trouble, and you believe him."

Chapman put his hands down on Uncle Felix's dressing table. He had gone quite gray in the face. I had that sick feeling in my stomach again, worse than ever. I wanted to get out—of the room, of Fallingford, of the whole case, from beginning to end. I wanted to go home.

"But, Chapman, you know Daddy! He never understands how important something really is, and he never knows what's good for him. Only remember last year, when he thought that he could make a saving by ordering kippers in bulk and then he ate five at once and they were off and he nearly expired? This is just like that. I'm sure that whatever you saw didn't really have anything to do with Mr. Curtis getting murdered. If you only told us what it was, we could tell the police that he's innocent. Otherwise they might suspect him!"

"No!" said Chapman, and he thumped his hand down so that Uncle Felix's cuff links rattled. "Miss Daisy, I *can't*. What I saw—it *proves* that he is guilty."

"What?" said Daisy faintly. She clutched at my elbow, and I squeezed her arm hard. Next to us, Beanie and Kitty were gasping.

"You can't tell the police," said Chapman, and he turned round and grasped Daisy by the shoulders. His fingers were all bent and knotted, but they seemed awfully strong. "On your honor as a Wells, you won't say a word."

Daisy bobbed her head, looking pale. At that moment Chapman was truly menacing.

"At the tea, I stood away from the table, as Lady Hastings had told me to. I saw the cups of tea being handed out. I heard Lady Hastings asking for a cup of tea for Mr. Curtis. And then I saw Lord Hastings pouring something into the cup. He thought no one had seen him, but as you know, Lord Hastings has never been very subtle. Then he gave that cup to Mr. Curtis. Mr. Curtis did not eat or drink anything else before he was taken ill. Nothing else could have been to blame. The tea was fresh when it was handed to your father. Lord Hastings is guilty of Mr. Curtis's murder."

"*No*," whispered Daisy. "It can't be! He—it must have been a mistake. How could you, Chapman? Let me go!"

She flung herself out of the room, and Chapman groaned and covered his face with his hands. I glanced back at him: his wrinkles were all heavy and his white hair downy-soft. He looked very small and sad, not at all like the smart, capable butlers in books.

I wanted to keep on believing Daisy—but despite what she said, the evidence was truly beginning to mount up against Lord Hastings. I didn't know what to think anymore.

Out onto the landing we went, and then I realized that there were new noises in the house. Heavy feet and deep voices, a whole lot of them—one with an ironic tone to it that I recognized from both my bad dreams and my better ones. My heart jumped.

Robin Stevens

"It's the police!" I breathed. "Inspector Priestley's here at last!"

"Oh!" said Beanie. "Now we'll be safe!"

All of a sudden I was simply dying to go downstairs. It made my fingers tingle. As soon as I saw his coat, I thought, and the back of his head, I would know that we were all right. Nothing bad could happen with Inspector Priestley there.

But Daisy was looking paler than ever. "I won't have us going to him," she said quietly. "I won't see him! If we simply go running down to the hall and pour out everything to him, we shall look like a lot of silly schoolgirls, and while we may technically be schoolgirls, we are certainly not silly. *That* is the point. *He* must come to *us*. After all, he has consulted us before. If he has any sense, he'll do it again. He knows who I—who *we* are—and this time more than ever, we are important. This is my house and my Detective Society."

"But, Daisy," I said, "if we don't tell him what we've found out so far, he'll work it out anyway. He's clever."

"That may be," said Daisy, "but—I can't just turn Daddy in as though he were anyone. You must see that, Hazel."

I looked at her. The crease at the top of her nose was scrunched so deep that it looked as though she had cut it. There were two little spots of red on her cheeks, and she was biting her lip so hard it almost hurt *me*. I believed in the police—but I also believed in Daisy.

"All right," I said. "We won't speak to Inspector Priestley. But, Daisy . . . promise, whatever happens—you won't blame me?"

"Hazel," said Daisy solemnly, "I would never blame you for anything. Unless, of course, it's your fault."

I made a face at her. There was something comforting about the fact that Daisy Wells, even in such a desperate situation, could still make a joke.

Robin Stevens

T hen out of his bedroom came the one person I had been hoping we wouldn't meet: Lord Hastings. I had been feeling sorry for him before, when I thought him being a suspect was all a mistake, but now, after what Chapman had said, I finally had to believe it. He could be the murderer—and if he was, I could not be sorry for him anymore. Instead, I suddenly felt rather frightened of him.

"Daisy?" said Lord Hastings, frowning and patting down his jacket. "Are you all right? You appear to have been upset by something. Here—I have my handkerchief somewhere . . . Oh dear, no, that's a sweet wrapper. And that's string. And that's—"

"Daddy!" said Daisy with a sob. "You're an idiot!"

Lord Hastings looked much discomposed. "Daisy," he said, patting at her hair in much the same way as he just had his jacket. "Daisy! Goodness me! What's all this then?"

"Mr. Curtis!" gasped Daisy. "Daddy, this is *serious*. You're in the most *awful* trouble."

And then Inspector Priestley came striding up the stairs.

I remember once, a long time ago, thinking that Inspector Priestley looked like a biblical angel coming to save us. But at that moment the stairway shadows fell on the planes of his face and the tails of his coat (he never seems to take off that coat, no matter where he is) and made him look rather wicked. He saw us, and his forehead wrinkled up. "Miss Wells and Miss Wong," he said. "Why am I not surprised that you are mixed up in this? And this time you've brought your friends."

"Erm . . . ," said Lord Hastings, twitching and staring about wildly—at the inspector's feet, at the space above his head and at the banister . . . "Erm, good morning, Inspector. I hope . . . That is, if you need any help, I'm sure you know where to find my wife. I must just excuse myself, however—things to attend to on the estate. Pardon me . . ." And he made a dive down the stairs. I heard his voice in the hall saying, "My goodness, what a lot of you there are! Pardon me, I must get by—"

"No one is to go in or out the house, sir," said a deep voice respectfully. "Chief's orders."

I felt sick. There was no getting out for any of us now. We had to see it through to the end. Poor Daisy!

We were alone on the landing with the inspector. Daisy

Robin Stevens

was refusing to look at him, but Beanie was gaping up at him in awe, and Kitty was considering him quite admiringly. I realized that he was looking at me.

"The Detective Society certainly seems to have increased in size since the last time I saw it," said Inspector Priestley. "I suppose it's too much to hope that you've been keeping your noses out of police business this time?"

"We don't have anything to say to you." Daisy glared over at the stuffed owl on its pedestal. I wished she would not be so rude—but I understood why she was. "Apart from to remind you that *we* solved the murder last time, not you, and you should be grateful."

"I *am* grateful," said the Inspector. "It's only that murders are quite dangerous, and I don't think your parents would like to lose you."

That made us all think of Lord Hastings, of course.

"*Parents!*" cried Daisy. "Much you know about it! Oh, go away. I wish you had never come."

"I come when I'm called, even through fire and flood," said Inspector Priestley, and gave us a wrinkled-up smile. "I don't mean to upset you. But if you do know anything, now's the time to say it. My men and I will be interviewing everyone this morning. We shall soon get to the truth."

"Oh no, don't!" said Beanie.

"*Beans!*" said Kitty, and kicked her shin.

The inspector raised his eyebrows. "I take it that you do

know something, then?" he asked. "Something not very nice?"

"None of your business," said Daisy—rudely, again. "We shan't say anything more. And we shan't be helping your investigation this time. You can't make us!"

"I wouldn't dream of making you do anything, but I am beginning to have a good idea of what is going on." The inspector's eyes went to the stairs down to the hall, and of course I knew exactly who—and what—he meant.

"Oh!" I said in horror.

"Unfortunately, the law is the law," said the inspector. "It can't be stopped because someone asks me to, no matter who that someone is."

I stared into his face, long-nosed and serious. I wanted to tell him everything, but I also wanted to be loyal to Daisy. I felt utterly torn. Then—"Come on, everyone," said Daisy. "We're going upstairs. Let's leave the *inspector* to his investigation."

Robin Stevens

We sat in the nursery, miserably silent. Downstairs I could hear the police at work. There were loud footsteps, doors opening and slamming, and heavy voices. "Get Rogers to do it!" I heard. "No, the fingerprints . . ."

Fingerprints, photographs, measurements and statements—all the things the police could do, and we could not. What was the point of the Detective Society?

Daisy was sitting with her face to the wall, refusing to look round even when I poked her. Kitty and Beanie were leaning together, looking as exhausted as I felt. I wondered whether they were glad to be part of the Society now.

The nursery door opened, and we all jumped. "Come downstairs, girls," said Miss Alston. "The police want to see you."

"Kitty and Beanie can go," said Daisy, still not moving. "But if they know what's good for them they won't say anything. Hazel will stay here. We're protesting."

I opened my mouth and closed it again in defeat. Miss Alston raised her eyebrows—but she didn't argue. Kitty and Beanie went. I stayed. Hetty, looking distracted, brought us up a late breakfast on a tray. I ate mine, and then, when she didn't move, Daisy's as well. It would only have gone to waste otherwise.

I lay on my back on my hard lumpy bed and stared up at the peeling paint on the nursery ceiling. I felt horrible— wiggly and wrong—but all the same I could not help poking away at the case in my mind. It was like having a tooth that aches every time you prod it with your tongue—it hurts, but somehow you cannot stop doing it. I thought about Miss Alston being a policewoman, hired to catch Mr. Curtis. I thought about Mr. Curtis's nasty little book, with a record of everyone he had stolen from. And of course, I thought of Lord Hastings—shouting at Mr. Curtis on Saturday morning, handing him that teacup on Saturday afternoon, and standing on the stairs on Sunday, looking down at Lady Hastings lying on the floor. He must have done it—I could not really believe that it was Uncle Felix, and there was no one else.

The nursery clock chimed midday, and all of a sudden I couldn't stay still any longer. It was a very Daisy-ish feeling to have—but Daisy wasn't being very Daisy-ish at the moment, so I had to take her place.

"Come on," I said to Daisy. "Get up."

Robin Stevens

"Go away," Daisy said.

I took hold of her shoulder—not very gently—and dragged her backward off her bed. She tipped over with a yelp and a rather unladylike word. "Hazel!" she said. "What's gotten into you?"

"I can't bear it," I said. "Sitting here, waiting. Can't we at least *do* something?"

"There's nothing to do," said Daisy. "But . . . Oh, very well."

We went out onto the landing, and saw that the door to Bertie and Stephen's room was open. Because that distraction was as good as anything, we peered inside and found Bertie huddled up on his bed, tinkling away on his ukulele. Stephen was nowhere to be seen.

"Oh," said Bertie when he saw us. "It's you. I'll play you a song. Look. *Wiiith my little—*"

"I don't want a song," said Daisy.

"No," said Bertie, stopping mid-jangle. "I don't much, either."

I could tell that Bertie was almost as upset as Daisy. I had never heard him being so nice before. "Where's Stephen?" I asked.

Bertie waved his ukulele. "Downstairs. Being interviewed, I think. Rotten weekend for him. Brought up bad memories. You know his father left his mother?"

I nodded.

"His mother took up with some filthy scoundrel who ran off in the middle of the night with half the things from the house. Jewels and paintings and so on. Mr. Bampton lost his job in the crash. The family had no money to fall back on and . . . he ran away to escape his creditors. Stephen and his mother were left to pick up the pieces. Stephen thinks his father was some sort of wronged hero, but *I* don't know. Bad form, I say, leaving your family like that," said Bertie, with a flare of his usual temper. "A Wells would never do it." Then he jumped and looked guilty, as though he'd just heard what he had said. "Er . . . sorry. I didn't mean Mummy—"

"You might as well have," Daisy said, scowling. "I don't care. Everything's *ruined*."

There was a noise downstairs—shouting. We all stiffened and pretended we couldn't hear it. I looked around the room desperately for something else to fix on—and then I saw, sitting on the battered old chest of drawers next to Stephen's empty bed, a book. It was a thin, cheap volume of poetry, and I went over and flicked through it. I was hardly even glancing at the words—until my fingers stumbled over a torn page.

When, from behind that craggy steep till then
The horizon's bound, a huge peak, black and huge,
As if with voluntary power instinct,
Upreared its head. I struck and

Robin Stevens

The rest had been ripped out. I put my hand in my skirt pocket and pulled out the piece of paper I'd been carrying about all weekend.

struck again,
And growing still . . .

It was a perfect match.

All the things in my head—the jumble of nearly right details that had all been fighting against each other and refusing to add up—suddenly trembled and spilled over and came back together again in a perfectly neat line, like the right answer in an exercise book.

"Bertie," I said very quietly, "whose book is this?"

"What?" asked Bertie, distracted. "That? Oh, that's Stephen's. The rubbishy poetry we're studying next term. Did he tear out a page? He must hate it even more than I do. He's usually boringly careful with his things."

I didn't even need to look over at Daisy to know that she had frozen. My heart was beating fast, fast, and I could hardly breathe. *The page.* The page the murderer hid the poison in before they tipped it into Mr. Curtis's cup. It was a page from one of Stephen's books.

"Bertie," said Daisy, "does Stephen use the servants' staircase? And does he know about the keys in the umbrella stand?"

"Eh?" asked Bertie. "You say the *oddest* things sometimes."

"Bertie, you prize idiot, will you answer me? Have you shown him the way down the back stairs?"

"Of course I have," he said. "I showed him as soon as we arrived. He can get down like a cat. He knows about the keys, too—I used them to get into the kitchens last Wednesday night, after the rest of you were all asleep."

I remembered how we'd ruled Stephen out of the second crime. We had heard him come clattering down the creaky front stairs from the nursery floor—but of course, of course, he could have crept down to the second floor on the servants' staircase. They come out just opposite the main stairs, so he could have come up behind Lady Hastings without her noticing, pushed her and then, in those ten quiet seconds, slipped upstairs again, before coming back down the front way, loud enough for everyone to hear. I felt sick. Could it really be? Stephen was so nice, and kind, and good—*and his father had left him because his mother ruined them. She took up with a scoundrel who stole all their things.* I remembered what he had said to me last night. *You're quite safe. Bertie and I—we won't let anything happen to the four of you. I can promise that.*

I pulled the crumpled notebook out of my skirt pocket and thumbed through it, back much farther than we had been looking before. And then I found it.

Robin Stevens

Bampton. Visited house 10.1.1928: a rich lot of jewels, worth hundreds, and some gorgeous paintings. Lovely wife happy to assist, practically handed them over. Took the lot—and husband's gold watch for luck. In the money!

The whole awful story was in those notes. The watch—it had been Stephen's father's. The man Mrs. Bampton had taken up with had been Mr. *Curtis*. Of course, when Stephen came to the house and saw Lord and Lady Hastings rowing, and Mr. Curtis sliding in between them, he must have felt as though it was happening again. He would have recognized Mr. Curtis, but after almost seven years, Stephen would look very different to the little boy Mr. Curtis had met. And Mr. Curtis had even flashed around Stephen's father's watch like a sort of trophy! I imagined someone boasting about hurting my father—and I could see that it might make me desperate to pay them back for what they had done. Right or wrong would hardly come into it. It would be family.

But as I thought that, I realized that there was another family in an even worse way than Stephen's, and it was all his fault. He had pushed Daisy's mother down the stairs and almost killed her, and because he had not owned up to killing Mr. Curtis, her father was suspected of the crime and might be in the most terrible trouble.

The thought of Stephen being the murderer made me

shake all over with horror and confusion—because he was *good*, I kept telling myself, *good*, and how could a good person do something so bad?—but Daisy and her family were innocent. They hadn't done anything. We had to save Lord Hastings, even if it meant hurting Stephen. I had to forget my feelings and be a detective.

"Daisy," I said frantically. *"The watch!"*

Of course, she understood me at once. Her nose went up like a dog on the scent, and she leaped forward.

"What is it?" asked Bertie, angry and confused, swinging his head from side to side. "What's up?"

Daisy ignored him. She went rootling through Stephen's chest of drawers, throwing aside much-darned socks, threadbare handkerchiefs, and carefully mended trousers. There was more evidence of what Mr. Curtis had taken from him, I thought, and felt sick with despair.

"Squashy! Hey! Put that down! Squashy, you heathen, leave it!" Bertie dived toward Daisy furiously. "Stephen's *things*, Squashy! What are you—"

But now Daisy had discovered Stephen's bathrobe, hanging up at the end of his bed, and wriggling her hands into the pockets, she yelped in triumph and pulled out . . . Mr. Curtis's watch.

There it was, and there was our final piece of evidence. Stephen was guilty.

Robin Stevens

And as I understood that, all over, like being pushed into a cold bath, we heard the most furious roaring in the hall below us.

"Daddy!" cried Daisy. "Quick, oh, quick!"

I didn't even hesitate. I ran downstairs after her.

We arrived halfway through a struggle. Lord Hastings was wriggling like a fat fish in the grasp of Inspector Priestley and the tall policeman, Noakes, while Rogers stood aside looking nervous. Beanie was crying, and Beanie's father—who must have arrived while we were upstairs—was glaring about furiously, as though he couldn't believe his eyes. Aunt Saskia was wringing her hands. Lady Hastings stood with her lips pressed together, leaning her bandaged head against Uncle Felix, who had one hand clenched around her shoulder. Miss Alston stood with her arms crossed, her face impassive. And Stephen . . . Stephen hovered in the shadows beside the library door, face white and drawn. How could I have not seen how suspiciously he'd been behaving? I wondered. How could I not have noticed before?

"Unhand me!" bellowed Lord Hastings. "UNHAND ME, I SAY! I had nothing to do with this—nothing—why won't you believe me? I . . . I— Chapman, *help* me!"

Chapman looked as though he wanted to weep. He stood hunched up and shaking. "Sir," he said. "I . . . I can't—"

"Lord Hastings," said Inspector Priestley. "If you won't give me another explanation for how you came to hand Mr. Curtis a teacup that appears to have been poisoned, just a few hours before he died of arsenic poisoning, I shall simply have to take you into custody. You must see that. I am quite willing to believe that there has been a terrible misunderstanding, but I need the truth."

"The TRUTH?" roared Lord Hastings. "I've given you my WORD! Surely that means more than . . . I tell you, I had nothing to do with that man's death. FELIX, can't you do something? Call your man in London. This is an outrage. HELP me!"

"I'm sorry," said Uncle Felix softly. "I can't do that, old chap."

He thought Lord Hastings was guilty, I realized. Everyone thought he was guilty. But how could I blame them? I had thought so, deep down in my bones, until just a few minutes ago.

We had to say something, and quickly, but Daisy seemed to be stuck. I jabbed her hard in the ribs, and she came unstuck in a rush.

"No!" she said. "STOP! Daddy didn't do it!"

"I know you think so," said the Inspector calmly, "but

unless someone in this case can give me some *evidence* to the contrary—"

"But we *do* have evidence!" cried Daisy. "Lots! And we know who the real murderer was too! It wasn't Daddy, it was Stephen!"

Robin Stevens

S tephen staggered back against the library door. He looked frantically around the hall—and then stared straight at me. His eyes were huge and he shook his head pleadingly.

I felt dizzy, as though I were teetering on the top of a very high cliff. I thought I'd already made my choice, but here I was, having to choose all over again. Knowing that I never could choose anything else didn't make it any less horrible.

I was always criticizing Daisy for letting her imagination run away with her—and here I was, ignoring evidence because it didn't suit me, because I'd liked Stephen so much. I couldn't do it anymore. "It's true," I said. It came out in a whisper, and I had to clear my throat and try again. "It's true. We've got evidence."

"Please!" said Daisy to Inspector Priestley. "*Listen* to us. We helped you before, didn't we? *Please.*"

I never thought I'd hear Daisy saying *please* to anyone.

But even so, it might not have been enough—if Stephen hadn't made a break for it. He scrabbled for the library door, panting, and quick as a slap the inspector rapped out, "Hold him."

Rogers dived forward and wrapped his skinny hands around him, and Stephen gasped and sighed and stopped moving.

"Come downstairs. You have five minutes to present your evidence," Inspector Priestley told us. "I shall be timing you."

"It isn't true," shouted Stephen in the background. "It isn't true—it isn't—"

"Shh," said Rogers sternly. "Don't interrupt the chief."

"We don't need five minutes," said Daisy. "We've got a piece of evidence from Mr. Curtis himself—a notebook that shows that he tricked Stephen's parents and stole all their nice things and his father's watch. That's why Mr. Bampton left, and *that's* why Stephen killed Mr. Curtis, to get his revenge. We found the watch in Stephen's bathrobe, and the book on the upstairs landing—and we've even found the bit of paper he used to wrap up the poison before he put it in Mr. Curtis's cup. It was torn out of one of his schoolbooks. They all prove that Stephen is the murderer."

Everyone was staring up at us with exactly the same expression—as though they couldn't understand what their ears were telling them they'd heard. Aunt Saskia gaped like a fish. Chapman sat down on the nearest chair with a heavy thump. "Good heavens!" said Uncle Felix to Miss Alston. "I thought you were supposed to be keeping them busy with lessons?"

"ll right," said Daisy. "Let me begin."

We were all sitting in the library—Inspector Priestley had ushered everyone in there after we dropped our bombshell. All the chairs and tables were still shifted about, so that Lady Hastings could have space to convalesce, and seeing them again in their different places, with Lady Hastings sitting up like a queen in the middle of the room, suddenly made the whole scene feel very unreal. It was as though we had stepped sideways into another house entirely, where a different Wells family lived.

The inspector still had his cuffs on Lord Hastings—but Noakes was standing over Stephen, one heavy hand pressing down on his shoulder. Stephen looked like he wanted to weep—and I felt the same. I kept on thinking of him as my friend, and then remembering with a jolt that he was not my friend at all.

It made me sick, and angry, as though I had been tricked.

All the nice memories I had of him twisted up and went sour. I felt as though the person I was staring at was someone I had never met before.

I suppose, in a way, he was.

I was brought back to the present by Daisy elbowing me not very nicely. "Hazel!" she said. "I need you for the denouement."

"It's not a *denouement*," I said. "We're not in a book. We're only explaining what happened."

"Well, then," Daisy said, "I need you for that. Help me explain."

"Where are we?" I asked. As usual, Daisy was enjoying this part far too much. She is happiest when she is standing up and talking, and everyone else is sitting down and listening.

"I've just told them about how Mr. Curtis stole the Bamptons' things," said Daisy, "just like he was trying to do here! He was nosing around our antiques, and then we heard him trying to persuade Mummy to come away with him and bring her jewels."

"Stephen must have recognized Mr. Curtis—and if he didn't at once, he would have as soon as he saw him flashing his father's watch around," I agreed. "And then, when we were playing hide-and-seek, he saw Mr. Curtis trying to make Lady Hastings run away with him after tea. He must have felt as though everything was happening all over again—I could see that he was terribly upset. We ran down to the first floor and—oh! While I went into the library to look for Beanie and Kitty, he must have gone into the cupboard and scooped some of the arsenic powder out into the piece of paper ripped out of the book in his pocket."

I remembered Stephen running into the library after me on Saturday afternoon, flushed and out of breath, and felt sick with fury. That must have been the moment when he stole the poison—that was why he was late.

"It would have been easy for him to get it—it would only have taken a minute at the most," Daisy explained. "Then all he needed to do was wait for everyone to gather around the tea table before slipping the arsenic into a cup of tea.

"Stephen must have thought that his luck had come in when Mummy actually *asked* for tea for Mr. Curtis. He passed it on, knowing that it would still get to Mr. Curtis without him actually having to hand it to him. And of course, the person he handed it to was Daddy."

Something suddenly occurred to me. "But what was Lord Hastings doing, if he didn't put the poison in?" I asked. "I saw his face straight after he had handed the cup to Mr. Curtis—he looked so guilty! That's what Chapman thought too."

"An excellent question," said Inspector Priestley, "and one that I have certainly been wrestling with. Lord Hastings, would you care to explain your actions?"

Robin Stevens

Lord Hastings coughed. "I . . . ," he said. "I . . . I hardly think I need to explain myself! Er—could you simply take my word that what I did had nothing to do with the, er, murder?"

"Unfortunately not," said the inspector.

"Oh, come on, Daddy, don't be an idiot!" said Daisy. "Just tell us. We know that you do some terribly stupid things—we're all quite used to it."

Poor Lord Hastings! I thought. Now that I knew he was not a murderer, I could feel sorry for him again. Sometimes I do think that Daisy is terribly cruel to her parents.

A red flush spread across Lord Hastings's plump cheeks. "I . . . ," he said again. "I . . . er—well, if you must know, I tipped salt into Mr. Curtis's cup before I handed it to him."

Chapman put his hands over his eyes.

"George, whatever were you *thinking?*" cried Lady Hastings.

"Daddy!" shrieked Daisy.

"It seemed quite funny to me at the time," said Lord Hastings, trying to look dignified. "Of course, I see in retrospect that it might not have been quite . . . well—quite the thing to do. But there are some things that a man simply can't take lying down, and someone coming into his house and stealing his wife is one of them."

"Good heavens, George, nobody *stole* me," snapped Lady Hastings. "I'm not a rug or a vase. I can do what I like."

"I know," said Lord Hastings. "I do *try* to understand. But . . . it was rather difficult this time. I hope you'll forgive me."

Lady Hastings sniffed.

"But, Daddy, if that was it—you've had everyone thinking you were guilty of *murder*! Look, Chapman's *crying*, poor thing."

"I certainly am not," Chapman said quickly, wiping the wet off his face. "Do forgive me—I was yawning. I must be tired."

"Er . . . ," said Lord Hastings again. "Yes. Well. I—I apologize."

Daisy rolled her eyes. "*Anyway*," she said, "then Mr. Curtis drank the poisoned tea and expired. Stephen must have felt pleased. But then he realized that he'd forgotten something. The teacup was still in the dining room, full of arsenic, and if the police were called in, they'd find it at once—with his fingerprints on it. The watch was also there, and of course he wanted that too, as it was his by rights. He waited until the house had gone quiet, pinched the keys from the umbrella stand, and then went into the dining room to clear up the cup and steal Mr. Curtis's watch. Quite by mistake, *we* disturbed him while he was still in the room."

I looked over at Stephen and shuddered.

"When we ran out, he must have stuffed the cup and

watch into his dressing-gown pocket, locked the door again, put the keys back in the stand and gone upstairs. Then all he had to do was slip into the kitchens the next day, while Mrs. D. and Hetty were out of the room, and put the cup back with the washing-up. They noticed it, which wasn't part of the plan, but of course they had no idea who had put it there. And we didn't either."

"When Mummy was pushed, we thought we could rule Stephen out. He had no motive that we could see and he was up on the third floor—we heard him come thumping down after she fell and Uncle Felix raised the alarm. But of course, he must have crept down the servants' stairs, shoved Mummy, dashed back up again and then come down by the front stairs, innocent as anything. He must have thought that when she talked to the police she would tell them something that might incriminate him . . . But how *could* you?" she asked, turning suddenly on Stephen. "Mr. Curtis really was a criminal, but Mummy never did anything to you. She didn't deserve to be almost murdered!"

Stephen shook his head. "I thought . . . ," he said. "I thought Lady Hastings was Miss Alston. She'd spoken to me earlier that day—she threatened me, and I realized that she suspected me. It was so dark at the top of the stairs, and she was standing with her back to me. I would *never* have pushed Lady Hastings if I'd known."

Lady Hastings looked outraged—and, I thought, slightly

put out. Just like Daisy, she likes to be the reason for every-thing. "Really, I don't believe that for a moment. You wanted to murder me!" she said. "And after I invited you into my home!"

"Never mind all that," said Uncle Felix smoothly. "I think we've heard enough. Inspector, don't you agree?"

A look passed between them, and Miss Alston caught the tail of it. She straightened her blouse, cleared her throat, and said, "Indeed."

Of course, I realized. Miss Alston really *did* know Uncle Felix. If she was a policewoman, and Uncle Felix was—whatever he was—they must both be on the side of the law, with Inspector Priestley. That was why Uncle Felix had not wanted to call in the police. He knew that they were not needed—there was an officer already in the house. I wondered whether Inspector Priestley had known all along, or had only been told when he arrived at Fallingford—for it was clear, from the looks he was giving Uncle Felix and Miss Alston, that he knew now. They must be desperate to cover up the truth of who Miss Alston was and what she was doing in the house. Daisy narrowed her eyes, glaring at them, and for a moment I thought she was going to say something. For once, though, she seemed to decide that it was best to stay quiet. I was glad.

"And that's really it, you see," she went on, turning to the inspector. "That's how Stephen did both crimes. The evidence is all there—the page, the hook, and the watch. So, do you believe us? Do you? You must! It all makes sense!"

Inspector Priestley's forehead was the wrinkliest I had ever seen it. "I . . . ," he said. "I *do*, as a matter of fact. Mr. Bampton, do you have anything to say for yourself?"

Stephen opened his mouth emptily. His voice, when it came out, was empty too, all hollow. "I am sorry," he whispered. "I'm sorry about Lady Hastings. I didn't mean to hurt her. And I would never have hurt anyone else."

I suddenly knew exactly what I wanted to say to him. "That's not true," I said. "You weren't going to hand yourself in, were you? You would have let Daisy's father be punished for what you did. And me—you made me think that you were *a good person*. How could you?"

"I thought I was," said Stephen miserably.

I think that was the first true thing he had said to me all weekend.

VIII

After that, Beanie's father rushed Beanie, weeping, and Kitty, eyes all goggly with shock and excitement, out of the door. He started the car, face thunderous, as Chapman loaded the cases into the trunk.

Daisy pulled us all into a huddle for one more hasty conversation. "You mayn't say anything," she muttered to Kitty and Beanie. "Not *anything* about the Detective Society or its part in this. Deadly secret, remember? We *swore*."

"But—" Kitty began.

"Kitty Freebody, I have told you before that I know medieval tortures and I will use them *all* on you if you so much as breathe a word of any of this. This is *important*!"

"Oh don't!" cried Beanie. "We won't! You know we won't!"

"*You* wouldn't," said Daisy, "but Kitty might. She *talks*."

"All right, all right," snapped Kitty. "I won't."

"I don't ever even want to think about it!" said Beanie. "Poor Mr. Curtis! Poor Stephen! Murder is *awful*."

"Thank you, Beanie," said Daisy, rolling her eyes. "So, Kitty. You won't talk? If you don't—you can stay members of the Detective Society. Minor members, of course, but it's an *honor*, see?"

"I told you I'll stay mum. But I want a badge."

"If there ever are badges," said Daisy grandly as Beanie's father ground the engine and glared at us, "you may have one."

Beanie and Kitty piled into the car; it crunched wetly down the drive, and then they were gone. It made me feel homesick again—though I was still not sure for where, I did know that I desperately wanted to follow them away from Fallingford.

After that Aunt Saskia got into her little car, shedding several scarves and a silver teaspoon in the doorway. She tried to kiss Lady Hastings and missed—or rather, Lady Hastings jerked away.

Then Stephen was taken away as well. Daisy and I watched out of the second-floor window—and though the monkey-puzzle was the same as ever, and the gravel drive, the whole world felt different. Now Stephen was below us, being pushed into the black backseat of the police car. Daisy had her arm round my shoulder and her most scornful expression on her face.

"He shouldn't have thought he'd get away with it," she said.

"He nearly did," I pointed out.

"What he was going to do to Daddy—letting him be arrested!" said Daisy furiously. "What he did to you!"

"He didn't do anything to me," I said quickly. "What about Bertie?"

"Up in his room. He hasn't even been playing his ukulele, so I know it's bad."

"They were best friends!" I said. "I mean, if boys have best friends. Imagine, having your best friend trick you like that."

"Well, I never would," said Daisy, squeezing my shoulder. "And I should think you'd notice if I tried to, anyway. You're far cleverer than Bertie is."

I didn't feel very clever, then. I didn't feel much of anything. My thoughts were all in a tangle. Stephen had nearly got away with it. We had only solved the case by the oddest, rarest chance—a few minutes more and it would have been Lord Hastings being driven away in that police car. In that moment I wished that I had never come to Fallingford.

Robin Stevens

IX

Inspector Priestley had not left with Stephen. He was still in the house, and somehow I felt very shy. I tried to keep out of his way—but it was no good. We were summoned to the library by Hetty, who looked very excited and curious, and when we arrived, there were Uncle Felix, Inspector Priestley, and Miss Alston, standing in a very serious semicircle. The sight made my stomach wobble.

I was not *afraid* of Miss Alston anymore exactly, now that I knew who she really was and that she was not a murderer—but I had no idea how to behave around her. I was still nervous of Uncle Felix, though. He seemed so important and official that I didn't like the idea of being noticed by him, and I still couldn't guess what he was thinking. And then there was Inspector Priestley. I wondered if he was cross that we had tried to hide the fact that we suspected Lord Hastings from him.

They didn't speak, and I didn't know what to say. Daisy, of course, had no such scruples.

"Hello," she said, her chin going up. "Hetty told us you wanted to see us. I suppose we can spare the time. What do you want to say?"

Uncle Felix screwed in his monocle, fixing us with his eye—and then he smiled. "Daisy," he said, "you are incorrigible. Good of you to grant us an audience. Yes, we want to speak to you."

I must have looked nervous, because the inspector said, "Don't worry. You aren't in trouble."

"Well, of course we aren't," said Daisy. "We solved the murder for you *again*. I should think we deserve medals."

"Indeed you do. You solved the murder," said the inspector, "and in your usual fine style. I don't doubt that we shall be able to get a conviction. However . . ."

"However," Uncle Felix put in smoothly, "we need to have a word about certain *other* facts that you discovered, which have nothing to do with the murder."

"Such as Miss Alston being a policewoman?" asked Daisy. She seemed thoroughly delighted to be able to annoy her uncle again without worrying that he might be a murderer.

"*Yes*, Daisy," said Uncle Felix. Miss Alston shifted and coughed discreetly. "And what we must ask you now is that you do not pass on that knowledge to anyone else. It is most

306   *Robin Stevens*

important that Miss Livedon—which, as I think you know, is Miss Alston's real name—is able to continue working on cases such as this without being compromised."

"Of *course* we wouldn't," said Daisy, rolling her eyes. "We're absolutely discreet, aren't we, Hazel?"

"We wouldn't ever," I said, nodding as hard as I could. "I promise."

"Good," said Inspector Priestley, and he smiled at me in a way that I knew meant he was really glad. I felt comforted.

Miss Alston—Livedon—smiled at us too. Although she was still in her dull, frumpy clothes, she somehow looked less like a governess and more like a real person, and I suddenly wondered if *I* could be like Miss Alston someday. Of course, that was silly. Miss Alston had to be able to fit in to do her job, and wherever I go I stand out as utterly different. All the same, I couldn't help imagining it.

"Miss Livedon came down to Fallingford on my orders," said Uncle Felix. "From time to time we collaborate with the Metropolitan Police."

So *he* was M, I thought. Everything was falling into place. There had been something about that letter—the person who wrote it seemed to know both Miss Alston and the Wells family. It made sense that Miss Alston had been working for Uncle Felix—doing whatever it was exactly Uncle Felix did. I wondered if he would ever be less mysterious to me—and suspected that he would not.

"We had been watching Mr. Curtis for some time—we were wise to his schemes—but we needed a few more pieces of evidence to close the case. We hoped that having a policewoman on the scene would help—Margaret had told me that her dear new friend Mr. Curtis was invited this weekend, and I knew I had to act. Unfortunately, he realized what Miss Livedon was up to on Saturday morning, and being the sort of person he was, it only made him more determined to outwit us. She and I were discussing whether we should bring him in when the murder happened—and then we knew that we had to keep our part in the case quiet. I suppose you thought it might mean I was guilty . . ."

I gulped uncomfortably. "Never seriously," said Daisy. She really *is* a good liar. "When we discovered Miss Alston's police badge, of course, we understood everything."

"I must admit," said Uncle Felix, "you're both very clever girls."

"Give it twenty years and they'll have you out of a job," said Miss Alston, smiling at him. "Girls, it's been a pleasure to teach you, and to be suspected by you. Criminals ought to beware."

"Thank you," said Daisy. "So they ought."

I decided that I liked Miss Alston—or rather, Miss Livedon—very much indeed.

We went upstairs—and as we passed Mr. Curtis's room,

Robin Stevens

we saw that its door was hanging open and the windows had been thrown up. Fuzzy bluish day glowed through it, and it made the whole house feel lighter. The body had gone.

The Case of Mr. Curtis seemed really to be over at last.

Very soon my father heard about what had happened. He called Fallingford on a line that hissed and rustled, and I had to listen to a lot of very upset shouting down the phone. I tried to explain that I was quite all right now, because the murderer had been taken away.

"But *another* murder, Hazel!" cried my father, sounding as though he was very far away and upside down. "How do you find these things? It's that friend of yours, Daisy. I don't like her."

"It's not her fault that someone was murdered in her house!" I said.

"I can't hear you. I said, I don't like her, and I don't like all these murders. I want you safe. Do I need to come over and be with you for the next holiday?"

"NO!" I shouted.

"I think I ought to. Yes. I will. I'll take you traveling. I DON'T LIKE that friend of yours—did you HEAR me?"

"NO!" I shouted again, and then the operator cut us off.

The day before we had to go back to Deepdean for the summer term, Daisy and I had a telephone conversation with the inspector. Hetty called us to the phone as quietly as she could—Daisy's father was still not at all fond of the police, and we knew that he wouldn't like Inspector Priestley contacting us.

"Mr. Bampton's in prison," said the inspector. I knew he would be—but all the same it gave me a horrible jolt. I almost dropped the receiver, and Daisy had to catch it for me. "He's awaiting trial. Because he's seventeen, he'll be tried as a minor—he won't face the death penalty."

I felt quite dizzy for a moment. I discovered that, although I still couldn't forgive Stephen for what he had done, I didn't want him to be hanged for it. I suppose that makes me terribly weak—but there it is. I was glad.

"Oh," said Daisy, as though she had just been told that the weather would be cloudy tomorrow. "I see. And I suppose you've taken all the credit again?"

"What do you take me for, Chief Inspector Wells?" asked Inspector Priestley, and even in his tinny phone voice I could hear his laughter. "There's a line in my official report that reads, *Acting on a tip-off from schoolgirl detectives Daisy*

Wells and Hazel Wong, I arrested Stephen Bampton and solved the case."

"Really?" cried Daisy.

"*Not really,*" I said, coming back to myself with an effort. "It's a joke."

"No, not really," the inspector echoed, "but you are both mentioned, although not by name. I've credited you as far as I can. I'm extremely grateful—you saved me from making an enormous and costly mistake. Arresting Lord Hastings for a crime he didn't commit! I'd have never heard the end of it."

"I think this time we *certainly* ought to get medals," said Daisy, grinning at me over the receiver.

"They're in the post," said the inspector. "Now I must go. Keep up the good work. You really do have a most successful Detective Society."

I thought he was joking about the medals, but it turned out I was wrong. That very afternoon, the post brought a fat parcel addressed to *Miss Wells and Miss Wong.* Daisy scrabbled it open and shook it, and onto her bedspread rolled four shiny silver badges. They said DETECTIVE on them, and Daisy squealed with excitement. She pinned hers to her blouse, and it winked up at me ferociously.

"Now we're really proper detectives," she said with a sigh of happiness.

There was a movement in the doorway, and I saw Bertie

standing there. He was looking at Daisy and her badge, and his face was quite blank. Then he turned away and shut the door.

I couldn't quite bring myself to wear mine after that. I stuffed it down at the bottom of my small trunk and left it there.

On Saturday morning we were down early, ready to be driven back to school. Our things had been packed by Hetty, and now Mrs. Doherty was fussing over us in the hall, trying to fit just one more cake into my small trunk and one more murder mystery into Daisy's.

"Perhaps you ought to stick to *reading* them for the moment," she told Daisy. "I think you've *experienced* quite enough to last you a lifetime."

"Hmm," said Daisy, narrowing her eyes and staring off into the distance thoughtfully.

Then the door from the garden banged open, and Lord Hastings was standing there in his Barbour jacket, Millie and Toast Dog surging around his boots. There had been a sort of ceasefire since the end of the case. Lord and Lady Hastings were talking again—carefully, and with many pauses, but talking all the same. None of us wanted to even breathe in case we jinxed it.

"Daughter!" he said. "Daughter's friend!" For a moment it was as if we were back at the beginning of the holiday again, and none of the dreadful things had happened.

"Hello, Daddy," said Daisy. "We're off to school."

"So you are," said her father, walking toward us. Then he paused and rubbed his chest thoughtfully. "Probably a good thing," he added at last. "This house—not exactly the right place for you at the moment."

"*You'll* be all right," said Daisy, and I couldn't tell whether she meant it as a question or not.

"I always am," said Lord Hastings. "Things have a way of working out." He paused again, bouncing on his toes, and then stuck out his hand toward Daisy. Daisy took it very daintily—and then, all of a sudden, threw herself forward and wrapped her arms around his neck.

"Steady on," said Lord Hastings. "Daisy, come now, you're far too old for this!" But as he said it, he lifted her up so her feet left the stones of the hall entirely.

"I'm glad you didn't kill anyone," said Daisy into his ear. "I'm glad you're good."

"So am I," said Lord Hastings. "It's a terrible relief, I can tell you. Do you know, I started to wonder if I had *ill wished* Mr. Curtis dead?"

Daisy burst out laughing. "Silly Daddy!" she said, letting go of him and leaping down to the ground again. "As if *you* could!"

"And you could?" asked her father.

"I," said Daisy, "can do anything. And even though she doesn't like to mention it, so can Hazel."

She grinned at me, and after a moment I smiled back at her. Lord Hastings shuffled off toward the billiard room, thumping Toast Dog on his fat behind and sighing. I hoped he *would* be all right. At least he had Chapman, Hetty, and Mrs. Doherty to look after him.

"Good old Watson," said Daisy. She took my hand and squeezed it. "I'm glad you've been here this holiday. Don't tell anyone, but it would have been awful without you."

"You too," I said. And I decided that being friends with Daisy was worth all the murders in the world.

"Detective Society forever," said Daisy.

"Detective Society forever," I agreed.

As we shook hands, there in the hall, I felt happy again at last.

Robin Stevens

On Sunday morning, the last day of holiday before the summer term, I woke up in my narrow, lumpy bed at Deepdean. The window was open, and chilly April-morning air was gusting in and creeping under our blankets and sheets. Beanie whimpered and wriggled lower in her bed, Kitty snored, and Lavinia sighed and rolled over like a heavy whale. I could smell the breakfast porridge burning downstairs, and when I turned my head I saw my trunk gaping open, still only half unpacked. I knew I would be told off by Mrs. Strike when she came in and saw it. I sat up, my school pajamas scratching my neck and arms, and took a deep breath.

Daisy bounced up out of bed, throwing off her blankets in one wild movement, and waved at me. "Hello, Hazel!" she said. "Back to the boredom. Cabbage and Latin for miles, and no murder anywhere. Why are you smiling?"

"No reason," I said.

And just like that, I wasn't homesick anymore.

Daisy's
Guide to
Fallingford

J ust as we did in our last important case, Hazel has asked me to give an explanation of the more difficult words in her notes. I think Hazel is far too worried—but she did insist, and I do like to give in to her from time to time, just so she never knows what to expect.

Apoplectic—this means when you are so full of anger that it looks like you are about to pop.

Arsenic—a nasty poison that makes you die in disgusting ways. But because it is also in lots of household things, it is very easy to get ahold of, which is why so many murderers use it.

Automaton—another word for robot.

Blancmange—a wobbly dessert made from milk. It is sweet but dull, nursery food really.

Bluestocking—a clever lady who is more interested in books than she is in men, and not very good at hiding it.

Brick—a good sort of person, one who can always be depended on in a crisis.

Buck up—what you say to someone to remind them that although bad things do happen, it is important to carry on regardless.

Bunbreak—this is a school word that is nevertheless important in all parts of life. It means pausing what you are doing to have something sweet and delicious, like cake or cookies or buns.

Combies/combinations—a word for underthings that are purely functional rather than nice.

Convalesce—something that people have to do after they have been ill. It means resting until you are better.

Dysentery—a truly horrid illness where you can't keep anything in at all. In the end you shrivel up and die. Quite often, when people are poisoned with arsenic, the silly doctors mistake its symptoms for dysentery.

For a song—this is a slang term that means *very cheaply.*

Governess—a sort of teacher who gives lessons to girls at home, rather than in school. Mummy makes me have one each holiday, which is very tiresome.

Grain—quite apart from being a word for a part of wheat, it is also the way that doctors measure doses of poison.

Halloa—a shout that you give to someone far away, to make them notice you.

Hothouse—another word for conservatory, where you can grow flowers and fruits even in the winter.

India rubber—this comes from trees in the British Empire, and can be used to make bouncy balls and other useful items. It is very stretchy.

Kedgeree—a sort of food that is cold rice mixed up with fish and eggs and yellow spices. It sounds horrid, but is not.

Kipper—a sort of smoked fish. It smells very strongly and it is delicious, though Hazel does not agree with me about that.

Kleptomaniac—a sort of illness that some well-off people have, where they can't seem to stop pinching other people's things.

Pash—this is school talk for something that is rather difficult to describe—I suppose it's being in love, but different somehow, and so quite all right with everyone

Pigskin—a sort of leather, that handbags are made from. It is very practical.

Popinjay—this is an old word for parrot—but it is much nicer than parrot, I think.

Prep—our school word for homework. Grown-ups think that if we are given enough prep we will be too busy to get into trouble.

Raffles—a famous character from a book. He is a master thief, and very clever. I rather admire him, although Hazel thinks that very wrong.

Rowing—another word for arguing. Grown-ups do it very often.

Sardines—this is a game, where one person hides and everyone else goes to look for them. When you find them, you have to squash into their hiding place with them, so you end up squeezed together like sardines.

Semaphore—a way of communicating using flags. You wave your arms about in special ways and it spells out words, like a very large Morse code.

Shrimp—a word from our school for the girls in the lowest grades.

Tooth mug—the mug that you keep your toothbrush in, of course.

View-halloo—this is a hunting word, and it means that you have found the fox and are after it. It can also be shouted when you are being a detective, to show that you have reached the good bit in the story and are about to catch the murderer.

ACKNOWLEDGMENTS

All of the people in this book are absolutely fictional—but some real places and names have managed to creep in. Thank you all (you know who you are) for letting me make you part of Daisy and Hazel's world. Special thanks, though, go to:

Boadie and her family. Fallingford House would not exist without them—and it would not look the way it does without Boadie's truly unique map-drawing skills. Not many people would have included the family stuffed birds, but she did.

Amy and Emily, who introduced me to the real Millie and Toast Dog, two most exceptional animals. I have tried to remember them with the fondness they deserve.

And Saskia, aspiring Jessica Fletcher—I hope she will not see any connection between her real self and her fictional alter ego apart from the name.

As well as all of the wonderful friends and family members who were mentioned in the last book (I still love you all in exactly equal amounts), several people made a special contribution to the creation of *Poison Is Not Polite*:

The Goodes, as kind as their name, who gave me a place to stay and a space to write in the difficult first months when nothing made sense and every character was in five rooms at once.

My brilliant first readers: my mother, Kathie Booth Stevens; my crit partner, Melinda Salisbury; and my agent, Gemma

Cooper. You were all perfectly right, and the book is much better because of your extremely clever suggestions.

My editor, Nat Doherty, who has been fantastic at corralling my plot and encouraging *Poison Is Not Polite* to be the best and most food-filled book it can be. My publicist, Harriet Venn, for her enthusiasm in promoting the series, and Mainga Bhima and the whole Penguin Random team—any book is a collaborative effort, and I could not have done it without a single one of you.

Kristin Ostby, for all of the wonderful work she has done to bring my heroines to America, and the rest of the Simon & Schuster team, who have been so helpful and kind. Elizabeth Baddeley and the Simon & Schuster design team, for bringing my books to life with such wonderful covers.

Everyone who has, in so many wonderful ways, spread the word about *Murder Is Bad Manners*—especially the Blackwell's Oxford team, who have put their considerable energy and enthusiasm behind the book. You have all bowled me over, and I am inexpressibly grateful.

My parents, for their unending pride and love—you made me what I am, and I am very lucky to be related to you.

And finally, again, my agent, Gemma Cooper. You are a true fairy godmother. Here's to many more!

—Robin Stevens, April 2015